D1605917

WHEN ADAM MET JACK

G.A. HAUSER

WHEN ADAM MET JACK
Copyright © G.A. HAUSER, 2008
Cover art by Beverly Maxwell
ISBN Trade paperback: 978-1-60202-115-0
ISBN MS Reader (LIT): 978-1-60202-114-3
Other available formats (no ISBNs are assigned):
PDF, PRC & HTML

Linden Bay Romance, LLC
Palm Harbor, Florida 34684
www.lindenbayromance.com

First Linden Bay Romance publication: June 2007

Chapter One

"Turner, listen to me." Adam Lewis cupped the tiny cell phone to his ear so he could hear over the passing cars outside his home in Malibu. "I'm not going to say anything, but if I get subpoenaed by the cops, what the hell do you want from me?"

"Loyalty! I want fricken loyalty from my business partner, Adam! You fuckin' ingrate!"

Adam yanked the phone away from his ear quickly so he wouldn't go deaf. "Turner! Shut the fuck up and listen to me! I told you this would happen one day. You think all those pretty young men you molested— Turner?" When the line disconnected, Adam snarled in anger and stuffed the telephone into his pocket. Using his key fob to unlock the door to his BMW, Adam climbed in and started the car. Before he put it into drive, he checked an address he had in his pocket. Grumbling under his breath as Turner's arrogant remarks rebounded in his head, Adam put the car into reverse, backing out of his driveway.

Jack Larsen stood over his desk, the telephone to his ear.

"Come on, love, don't keep putting me off," Mark sighed. "It's a bit cheeky of you to keep saying no. Meet me for a bite. Please?"

"No…I have an appointment coming in in about ten

minutes," he checked his watch, "so I can't have lunch with you. Can I get back to you and check my schedule for a better time?"

"I'm getting very cross with this attitude, love. But I'll let you off this time."

"Okay. Bye, Mark." Jack hung up the phone. He couldn't get used to the fact that his gorgeous British best friend, Mark, was now shacked up with an ex-cop. The ex-cop who decided to switch careers and ended up falling for Mark when Mark started working for Parsons and Company. So they were lovers? So what?

But Jack never forgave Mark for loving another man. Under his breath, Jack muttered, "Don't torture yourself; it's ancient history."

"Jack?"

Jack turned to see his secretary hovering in the doorway. "Your ten o'clock is here."

Straightening his tie, Jack nodded. "Show him in. Thanks, Pam." He moved behind his desk and stacked a few pieces of paper into a neat pile. Jack waited while his secretary invited the man in, getting his first look at his new client. Tall, slim, neatly trimmed hair, sunglasses pushed to the top of his head, and a smart tailored outfit of snug black slacks and a button-down cotton shirt of gray and white pinstripes. Jack thought the man was very attractive.

"Adam Lewis?" Jack extended his hand in greeting.

"Yes. And you're Jack Larsen. Wow, you are fantastic."

That surprised Jack. It was an overt statement that possibly indicated Adam was gay. Jack gave Adam another quick once over. He knew little of Adam's need for a lawyer, let alone anything about his private life. "Have a seat. What can I do for you?"

Adam had just sat down in the leather chair across from Jack's desk when his mobile phone rang. Adam cursed under his breath, pulled it out and hissed, "Can't get a damn minute's peace." Shutting it off, he shoved it back into his pocket. "Sorry."

"No problem." Now that they were both quiet, Jack leaned his elbows on the desk in a relaxed pose, waiting.

Adam took a breath. "Look, this is the thing. I work for a talent agency with a guy named Jack Turner. He has a nasty habit of blackmailing the prettiest boys for sex in order for them to get parts. I hate to admit this, but I knew he was doing it and turned my back to the whole nasty business. Now one of the boys is going after him, and I'm afraid even though I didn't touch anyone, I'll be sunk."

"You want anything to drink? Coffee? Water?" Jack offered. Adam looked ready to snap.

"How about a bourbon?" Adam joked. "No, I'm all right. Look, Mr. Larsen, the shit may hit the fan, and I'm scared I'll be implicated and they'll think I was the one who was victimizing those poor guys."

"Why didn't you go to the police about it?" Jack hated men of power who abused young men, hated them.

"If I had? If none of the victim's backed my word, what then? Not to mention it's how most of these business transactions are done. Mr. Larsen, you're in law, you don't know what goes on with agents and wannabe stars. It's disgustingly common. It's vile, it's sickening, but it's more prevalent that you think. I just kept my nose out of it and went on with my business." Adam rubbed his face tiredly. "What the hell was I supposed to do anyway? First of all, most of the young men got fantastic parts as a result. Jack Turner is a powerhouse in the industry. There are some agents that get their dicks sucked and then give the poor fuckers nothing in return."

Jack thought he knew Adam's type. Money-grubbing. Using people to get what he needed. Nasty, self-centered.

"Why are you looking at me that way?" Adam asked.

Jack sat up in his chair. "So, I take it you came here to our law office for protection so you won't be implicated."

"Yes. I want advice on how to keep my tight gay ass out of jail."

"Are you willing to turn state's evidence against Mr.

Turner?"

"Yes. Look, I know what you're thinking. You think I'm some kind of monster that allowed this to happen."

Jack's top lip curled involuntarily.

"I'm not, Mr. Larsen. You'll meet Jack Turner. He scares the crap out of me. He's big, ugly, and vicious. The guy can ruin your career in one phone call. I just kept out of his way. I was wrong, all right? I admit it. I should have said something, but I have to make a fucking living in this town. You know? And I'm already shit scared my career will go down with his."

Reclining in his chair, Jack gave Adam another look. Gay, out, rich, and damn good looking. If the circumstances were different, Jack would ask him out. No, he wasn't pretty, he didn't have Mark's androgyny or Steve's machismo, but Adam Lewis was damn sexy.

"You're looking at me weird again." Adam met Jack's gaze. "Mr. Larsen, I'm sorry. I know everyone will hate me, shun me, put me in either isolation or jail, and I deserve it."

"Before we slap cuffs on you and cart you away, let me confer with two other attorneys on our staff. Jennifer Bernstein is the senior partner and has enough experience to get us in the right direction, and Sonja Knight is our expert criminal attorney."

"But I want you."

Jack blinked, then realized what Adam meant. "You will get me. I will be your council, but it doesn't hurt to get some advice or have a second chair."

"I know my judgment hasn't been very good up to now. You know, sticking it out with Turner. So, whatever you say, Mr. Larsen. I will defer to your decisions on this matter."

Jack took a last look into Adam's brown eyes before he left the office. "First of all, quit the Mr. Larsen bit. You can call me Jack. Okay? I'll be right back."

Adam watched Jack walk out. He was huge. The man could probably bench-press three hundred pounds. Jack's shoulders pressed at the material of his suit jacket. "Wow...wouldn't mind climbing on that for a while." Adam chided himself for his inappropriate timing.

A photo on Jack's desk drew Adam's attention away from his thoughts. Looking behind him first, Adam turned the frame around. It was a photo of Jack with his arm around an extraordinarily attractive man with long hair and brilliant green eyes. "Gay? You're gay?" Adam couldn't believe this masculine muscle-man was gay. "Gay and hooked up with a god. Holy shit. Nice one, Jack my boy."

Hearing noise behind him, Adam quickly set the frame down and pretended he was busy doing nothing.

Jack showed two women into his office. One was a gorgeous African American woman and the other was older and obviously attractive in her youth. Adam stood instantly as Jack introduced him to Ms. Sonja Knight and Mrs. Jennifer Bernstein.

Jennifer said to Adam in a calm voice, "We were wondering, Mr. Lewis, if you would mind moving to the conference room where we can be more comfortable."

"No. Not at all." As Adam walked behind Jack, he salivated at his tight ass and fantastic legs. Out of habit, Adam took his cell phone out of his pocket to check on his calls. His livelihood depended on his services, and he didn't want to lose all his clients over this incident.

Arriving in the conference room, Adam stuffed the phone back into his pocket, took a seat, and even though the women in the group were outstanding, Adam only had eyes for the blue-eyed, blond body-builder.

Sonja leaned over the desk to speak to Adam. "I know the district attorney well. Do you want me to get you immunity in exchange for your testimony?"

"Yes. If that's possible. Please." Jack was staring at him again. He wondered if Jack thought he was a monster. If they all did.

"Anything is possible," Sonja replied. "How much do you know about the encounters that Mr. Turner had with prospective and active clients?"

"Enough." Adam nodded. "I've never seen him do anything serious. I always left the room when he did since it made me sick. But I was there to see him make advances to the men and touch them like he owned them. He didn't mind doing that in front of me." Adam cringed at the memory.

Jennifer asked, "Did any of the men involved come to you for help?"

"No." Adam quickly glanced at Jack's face, then he answered Jennifer's question. "I don't know why they didn't. I couldn't have done anything to stop it. I suppose it does seem logical that one of them should have asked me if he did it to all the guys, or something."

Jack leaned closer to speak softly. "Are some of these well-known actors?"

"You kidding?" Adam laughed sadly. "Christ, he had them all. You know Ewan Gallagher? Remember him from that Murphy's Hero film? Ewan got so fed up with it, he headed back to London with his doctor-lover and gave up a promising career here in the States. I'm surprised he never pursued charges. But most men don't want to admit that they did that kind of thing to get a part, and the rest are just grateful for the starring roles and the chance at the big time." Lowering his voice, he added, "You realize how long Turner has gotten away with it?" No one answered. "Years. Thirty years. I'm telling you it is done in Hollywood and accepted as part of the contract and payment. It's sick and I hate it, always have. But who the hell am I? I'm just one working slob trying to pay his bills. You all probably think I should have gone to the police sooner, right?" He felt like the worst heel.

Jennifer spoke up, "No, Mr. Lewis. We understand the pressure you were under. It was up to the boys to make the move and to file. If you had said something and none of them came forward, then all you would have accomplished was losing your job."

"Exactly." Adam stared at Jack again. Speaking directly to that amazing blond, Adam asked, "Do you believe me?"

Jack shrugged. "I don't know. What if you went to one of the young men and said you'd support them. Would you have done that?"

Adam knew his torrid story was doing anything but winning over this hunk. And besides, Jack had a pretty boy to screw at home. "I don't know. I suppose I was waiting for one of them to ask me directly. You know, 'Hey, Adam, can you help me out here?'"

Sonja opened her notebook and lifted her pen. "Can you name anyone in particular that is involved? At this point, pre-trial, I don't know how much information the defense attorney for Mr. Turner is going to be willing to give. Most of that information is done in discovery, then we get a list of names, witnesses, statements, the works."

Adam had some ideas but was hesitant. "Look, Ms. Knight, I can give you the names of the young men who may have had bad experiences with Turner, but I know my clients. Unless they are the ones coming forward in this claim, they won't want the publicity. Think about it. Think of any of the top leading men in films coming forward and admitting that they had to suck a man's cock for their role. No one wants that. That's why it's taken so long for it to catch up to Turner."

Jack began to have second thoughts about his first impression. Adam was right. Which Hollywood icon, particularly the straight ones or the closet gay men, would come out to the press or the courts and say, "Yes, I sucked a man's dick for a part." It was one of those unspoken truths. An ugly little Hollywood secret that stayed that way, secret. Until one brave man decided enough was enough.

"I have a suggestion." Jack rested his elbows on the

table. "Can we place a discreet ad to lure more victims out of hiding? Maybe they can testify without revealing their identities? Anonymously. Just to bring more victims out and turn it class action."

"He'll settle," Adam butted in. "Turner will not go to court to tell anyone about his little obsession. I am telling you Turner will strike a bargain with the DA."

Jennifer shrugged. "We don't care if he settles, Mr. Lewis. But if there are a number of victims willing to testify, he'll be settling for time in jail. If it's one man's word against his, Mr. Turner will have a good chance at getting away with it."

Sonja asked, "Who's representing him?"

"A guy named Arthur Harris," Adam replied. "He's already called me to be a witness for the defense. I told him no way." At the drop of that name, all three attorneys looked at each other. "That name means something to you?" Adam asked.

"It does," Jennifer sighed.

"He's one of the toughest, sleaziest defense attorneys in Hollywood, Mr. Lewis." Sonja closed her notebook. "I've been up against him before. He's nasty. He makes the jury think whatever the suspect did, he did it because he had to, or that God told him to. It's as if he's claiming insanity without the defense of insanity on the book."

Adam looked at Jack, as if asking him what to do.

"We'll take care of you, Adam. Don't worry. Sonja and I will go speak to the DA and get them to tape an interview with you. Just tell them what you know."

"With immunity to prosecution?" Adam clarified.

"We can only answer that question after we speak to them." Jack looked at his two co-workers as if that were a sign they were finished.

The women stood and shook Adam's hand before they left the room. "Don't you worry about it, Mr. Lewis. We'll be here for you."

"Thank you, Ms. Knight."

Jennifer held out her hand next. "If you get worried, just call. We're here."

Adam tried to get their names correctly. "Thank you, Mrs. Bernstein. I really appreciate it." Adam watched them leave, noticing Jack standing as well. "Jack, wait."

As Jack paused, Adam peeked behind him to make sure they were alone. "It matters to me what you think of me."

"Why? It won't change the way I defend you."

Adam felt coldness in the pit of his stomach. "Still. I don't want you to think I'm one of those slimeballs like Turner. It makes a difference to me."

The comment intrigued Jack. Closing the door, he gestured for Adam to sit back down. Once they were next to each other at the large conference table, Jack asked softly, "I don't care for men like you. I've seen your kind before. You're the type to use and abuse." Pausing, he added, "You wanted to know. I'm sorry if it insulted you."

Adam's expression dropped painfully. "I didn't abuse anyone, Jack. I made a living. If anything, I did a lot to counteract the abuse Turner was giving them. I was there for them. I was. You have to believe me."

"Why is it so important to you what I think?" Jack sat back, watching Adam's expression carefully.

And as if the reply was agony, Adam rubbed his face, running his hand through his brown hair. "Okay. Honestly?" Adam straightened his back and made direct eye contact. "I think you are absolutely adorable. I know you are gay, or at least I suspect you are, and are most likely attached, but we're kindreds, Jack. I guess I hoped my damn lawyer wouldn't think I was as bad as Turner."

"What makes you think I'm gay?"

"That photo. There's a photo on your desk of you embracing a very pretty man. I'm sorry. Did I get it wrong? You just were holding one another in such a way. I've never seen a straight guy expose a photo of himself of that kind with another man, especially in an office environment. In my business it's the exact opposite, the gay ones hide in the shadows. I'm sorry. The last thing I wanted to do was offend you."

Jack knew that he shouldn't have put that photo on display. It was more his wishful thinking than reality. Mark wasn't his. Maybe he and Adam weren't so different after all. They were both living a lie.

Adam appeared confused by the lack of an answer. He probably expected to be informed he was wrong or told to mind his own business, anything but silence.

Finally, after what seemed like a long, uneasy pause, Jack replied, "Look, that guy in the picture, Mark Richfield, he's just an old friend I've known since college. I guess it is odd to have the photo sitting there." He made direct eye contact with Adam when he added, "But saying that…I am gay, and out." Adam's excitement was so obvious that Jack expected to be asked out on a date instantly.

"I knew it. Or at least I'm glad you are." Adam leaned closer to Jack. "It makes a difference to me somehow, Jack. I feel like I've got enough to deal with. This thing with Turner is killing me. I don't need my straight attorney cringing at the sight of my gay ass."

A chuckle escaped Jack's lips. "Believe it or not, I understand."

Adam touched the back of Jack's hand as it rested on the table near him. Jack raised his eyes quickly to Adam's.

In a sensual whisper, Adam said, "I don't know what's wrong with the guy in the photo. He must have been crazy to pass you up."

A chill washed over Jack's spine. Pining over Mark wasn't getting him anywhere. Looking for Mark's twin was equally impossible. And though he couldn't put his finger on it, there was something extremely sexy about Adam Lewis.

Adam struggled to read Jack's turquoise eyes. So much was passing through them it was difficult to pinpoint what was there. Pain from loss? The possibility of some good sex? What?

"Is there some code of ethics about dating clients?" Adam asked, his hand still in contact with Jack's warm skin.

"Yes and no." An ironic smile passed over Jack's lips.

"I like the yes part. Can we skip the no part?" Adam moved his fingers, caressing Jack's hand.

Jack peered over Adam's shoulder to the window that exposed them from the hallway. He removed his hand from Adam's. "Let's just see how the case goes. You're in no rush, are you? I mean, we have time."

Tilting his head in confusion, Adam asked, "What are you talking about? Time for what?"

"To date. Isn't that what you're implying?"

Covering his mouth to stop his laughter, Adam muttered, "You are amazing."

"Am I?" Jack blinked his bright blue eyes.

"Yes. A second ago you told me you are sickened by men like me. Did I do something to change your mind? Win you over? Are you trying to tell me we can date after this whole mess is through?"

"Maybe."

Adam sat back in the chair and gave Jack's enormous body a slow once over. "I sure as shit hope you and Ms. Knight strike a deal with the DA today."

Jack began laughing, but quickly controlled himself. "Christ, I don't remember the last aggressive wolf I've encountered. I can say it's been a while."

"Why? Are you kidding me? I find that hard to believe. Any gay man would drool over the likes of you, Jack Larsen."

"I don't go out much. I work here, exercise, sleep. You know."

"Don't you get hit on in the gym?"

"No. I have all my equipment at home. I don't go to a

11

gym."

Adam looked behind him at the movement beyond the plate glass, lawyers coming and going. "I'm keeping you from your work. Can we get together for lunch? We can call it strictly business."

"Sure." Jack rose up from the chair.

Before they left the privacy of the conference room, Adam asked, "You can make this nasty business go away for me, can't you?"

"I will try my best. Until we speak to the prosecutor and see what kind of a deal he'll cut, I have no idea."

"Okay. I get it. Oh, do you live alone, or with—"

A shadow passed over Jack's face. "No, I live alone."

"Oh." Adam was about to add, "good", but the devastated look held him back. "I suppose I should be going." Holding out his hand, Adam reached for a shake. When Jack grabbed it, Adam squeezed it tightly, hoping to convey his attraction, if his words hadn't already. "I'll prove to you I'm not a monster, Jack."

Jack responded wryly, "Except in bed?"

Adam roared with laughter. "Oh, man, I can't wait to get my hands on you, Jack Larsen. You are my dream man."

"It is flattering to hear you say that. Thank you, Adam."

"It isn't just flattery, Jack, it's lust."

Smiling in amusement, Jack opened the conference door. "I'll call you the moment I hear anything."

"Thanks, cutie. I'll be waiting."

Just to see him once more before he walked away, Adam looked back, finding Jack staring after him.

"Mr. Lewis?"

Adam turned around to address Jack's secretary. "Yes?"

"Sorry to bother you, but it's customary that we get a retainer from you for the services we'll be giving you."

"Oh, of course." Adam found his wallet. As he took out his credit card and handed it to her, he couldn't stop himself from looking back down that empty hallway, trying to get another glimpse of that tall, muscular blond.

Chapter Two

Jack sat on a weight bench in his workout room. Mirrors lined one wall, rock music blared loudly, Led Zeppelin's "Whole Lotta Love", as he prepared himself for another lift of the loaded weights. Tugging his leather gloves tighter over his hands, Jack took a deep breath, laying back and gripping the bar. Arching his back, he heaved two hundred and seventy pounds over his chest. He did ten repetitions, set the bar down, catching his breath.

"At it again, Mr. Larsen?"

Jack jumped at hearing someone in the room. "Give me back my key, Mr. Richfield, before I either die of a heart attack from your unexpected visits, or shoot you thinking you're a burglar."

Mark wandered in, looking at the equipment. "Oh, this is new."

Jack nodded. "Just bought it."

After checking it out, Mark sat on it, doing a few lifts with his legs behind the pads.

"Where's Steve?"

"On his way in. He has a habit of waiting for your gate to close. You know, forever the cop."

"I thought I said I would call you." Jack lay back down on the bench for another set of repetitions. Mark stood behind him to spot him.

"I know. You did. But Steve and I know you. You're too

shy to call. You keep harping on about being the fifth wheel."

Right before he lifted the heavy bar, Jack noticed the handsome Steve Miller enter the room.

Concentrating on his workout, his salvation to alleviate his stress, Jack gripped the bar and strained as he pressed ten more into the air. Mark helped him reset the weights back on the mounts.

Steve walked over to them and asked, "How much is on that thing?" When Jack didn't answer, Steve added it up. "Holy shit, Larsen! You're pressing two hundred and seventy pounds without a fucking spotter?"

Mark waved it off. "Are you kidding me? This is lightweight for He-man."

Jack knew they were trying to include him, being friendly, and they truly liked him, but he never felt comfortable around them. After all, Steve got the prize. Jack hated to be jealous, but he had loved Mark since college. A hell of a long time.

Standing, getting two more ten pound plates to load up the bar, Jack didn't make eye contact, but he could see them both staring at him through the reflection in the wall of mirrors. "What do you guys want?"

Steve reached for one of the metal plates and slipped it on the opposite end of the bar for Jack.

Mark said, "We wanted you to come out to dinner with us. Stop being such a fuddy duddy."

"You know I work out every night after I leave the office." Jack lay back down on the bench and stared at the ceiling.

"We can wait." Mark crossed his arms over his chest.

"I just started. Look," Jack tried not to get angry, "just go out without me."

"Jackie-blue!" Mark pouted. "We want you to come out with us."

Steve intervened, "Mark, if he doesn't want to…"

"No. I don't." Jack gripped the bar again, getting ready.

14

Instantly he seemed to have two spotters who doubted he could manage without them. Trying to ignore them and get on with his routine, Jack inhaled, roared as he lifted the bar off the mounts, pressing eight times up and down. Steve at one end, Mark at the other, helped replace the enormous load back on the machine.

"Holy fucking Christ, Larsen!" Steve gasped. "You are unbelievable. What's your maximum weight?"

Knowing Steve was genuinely trying to show an interest, Jack was loath to be nasty and tell him to fuck off. *Get over it, Larsen*! Jack chided himself for holding that grudge for so many months. Yes, he was happy for Mark when he found Steve. Yes, he even cheered for Mark and Steve at that horrible disaster of a wedding. He knew it was poor Mark's attempt at a heterosexual relationship with Sharon. But as the days wore on, and Mark moved into Steve's home, the pang of regret and loneliness surfaced.

"Three hundred and fifty," Jack said.

Steve appeared knocked over by the amount. "One time?"

"Yes."

Jack stood to get two more ten-pound plates. Steve rushed to help him.

In his sleek, feline-like way, Mark wrapped around one of the poles of another machine. "You'd want this powerhouse to back you on the streets, wouldn't you, Steve? If you were still a cop?"

"I'm so impressed. Christ, Jack, I don't know anyone who can do that. You're one strong mother-fucker."

Silently, Jack stuck the metal plate on the already loaded bar, wishing they would go away and let him work out in peace.

And Jack knew Mark knew him too well not to read that sign. "Okay, Jackie-blue, we'll leave you to it. But we will be back if you don't call."

Jack was trying to get used to Mark's new nickname for him. It seemed ever since Steve had come on the scene, he was now "Jackie" or "Jackie-blue". Nothing Mark did ever made any sense to him. "I should change my locks." Jack said it as a joke, but perhaps it wasn't a bad idea. Why did Mark still need a key to this house? He didn't live here anymore.

A look of obvious guilt passed over Steve's face. He moved closer to Jack and whispered, "I'm sorry."

Hearing it, Mark whacked Steve on the arm to shut up.

Lying back down on the bench, closing his eyes to stop the pain in his heart, Jack sighed, "It's okay."

"You…you want a three-way?" Steve asked.

Again Mark hit him.

Steve reacted to the blow. "What? I'm just saying—"

"I don't need a sympathy fuck. I can find my own sex." Jack held onto the bar again, rubbing his gloves over it to get a good grip. Waiting, seeing them both standing there ogling, Jack asked, "What now?"

"We just love watching you." Mark smirked, but it was in adoration.

"Fine." Jack psyched himself up, growling loudly to help him lift the enormous weight off the mounts. Four repetitions and the two men helped him rest it back on the machine. Standing, shaking out his arms, Jack began taking off the plates and unloading the bar. When Steve helped him, Jack announced, "I can do it myself."

Mark touched Steve's arm. "Come on. He's having a moody."

As they walked out of the room, Jack heard Steve say, "Did you see the size of his fucking arms?"

The Led Zeppelin CD had ended, the room grew quiet, and the sound of the front door closing reached his ears. After he had emptied the last of the weights from the bar, Jack sat down on the bench and covered his face with his hands.

Adam had his cell phone to his ear as he walked to the

parking garage to his car. "Yes…I know. No, it won't make any difference. I'm still the one getting you auditions."

"But I heard Turner is being indicted and you're not handling any—"

Rolling his eyes tiredly, he didn't know how many more phone calls like this one he could take. "No. I don't care what you heard. This won't affect your work. I promise. Look, Bill, I am still doing the job. Okay? I know where you have to go, who you have to see, I can get you your damn manicures, so stop worrying and trust me."

"Trust you?"

"Yes! Trust me!"

"But what if Turner—"

"Forget Turner. I'll be helping you from now on. Now, stop whining and give me the list of things you need me to do." With the phone tucked between his shoulder and his ear, Adam found his electronic notebook and began entering information into the calendar. "…yes, hair-cut, manicure, screen test, next Tuesday. Got it." Pocketing his mechanical gizmo, Adam leaned against his car and said, "Just don't worry. I'm here. I won't let you down." After he hung up, he rubbed his face in exhaustion, saying, "I need help. God, Turner, why did you do this to me. You stupid jerk."

Sitting behind the wheel of his car, Adam started hitting the buttons on his phone and made all the necessary appointments for his client. Checking his messages, he found more and more complaints and nervous voices as the rumor spread of Turner's coming indictment. "Right. I can't do this by phone." Starting his car, he headed home to type up a group email to all his clients. It was all he could do. And he needed to hire someone, fast.

Stopping in front of his home, Adam noticed a familiar car already waiting in his driveway. Behind the wheel was the nasty Mr. Turner.

"Shit." Instead of pulling in, Adam kept moving down

the street and parked, calling his lawyer.

"Bernstein, Larsen, Knight and Associates, how may I direct your call?"

"Jack Larsen, please. This is Adam Lewis."

"One moment."

Adam checked his rear view mirror in paranoia.

"He's out of his office, is this urgent?"

"Yes."

"I'll try his cell phone, hold please."

Tapping his fingers on the steering wheel, Adam kept his eyes on the mirror just in case Turner had seen him pass.

"Hello, Mr. Lewis?"

"Yes?" Adam asked.

"Mr. Larsen asked if you could call his cell phone directly, do you have the number?"

Adam rechecked the business card Jack had given him. "Yes. I do. Thanks." He hung up and dialed again.

"Adam?"

"Jack, look, I came home just now and Turner is parked in my driveway. What should I do?"

"Are you afraid of him?"

"Yes! Are you kidding me?" Adam looked in the rearview mirror again.

"Call 911."

"Really? Call the cops?"

"What do you want me to do?"

"I don't know. Come here and tell him to leave me alone."

"The cops can do that. Meanwhile, I'll write up a restraining order. He's harassing a witness. The courts don't take kindly to that."

"Jack, please, where are you? Can't you just stop by?"

After a pause, Jack said, "Okay. But call the cops now. You hear me? That way if Turner gets mean they'll be there to stand by."

"How long will it take you to get here?" Adam checked his watch.

"Where are you again?"

"Malibu."

"Right. I remember. Give me your address once more."

Adam did, then almost had heart attack when a Cadillac drove by, but it wasn't Turner's.

"Okay," Jack said. "When you hang up, call 911 and tell them to stand by with you until I get there."

"Okay. Thanks, Jack. I mean it. You're a life-saver." Adam hung up, then inhaled for courage and dialed 911.

Parking his maroon Jaguar behind the patrol car, Jack could already see a confrontation in action. Hopping out, he hurried over to the group to hear what was being said.

"All right, calm down," one of the patrol officers demanded as the shouting escalated.

"There," Adam pointed to Jack. "That's my lawyer. Jack Larsen."

Jack approached the four men and got his first look at the infamous Mr. Turner. Revulsion didn't begin to describe what he felt for the creature. A soggy cigar in his lips, pock-marked skin from bad acne in his youth, greasy black bumpy hair, a pointy dyed jet-black goatee, and a neck so thick his gold link chain all but vanished in the folds. On each of Turner's fingers was a gold ring clustered with diamonds, a golden Rolex with a diamond dial on his wrist. The cologne smell that was coming off the man Jack could catch from five feet away.

"Officer…" Jack read the man's name tag, "Officer Smith, my client is a witness against this man and I have just applied for a restraining order to keep them apart."

"What?" Turner shouted. "A witness against me? You son-of-a-bitch! After all I did for you?"

Adam cringed.

"Mr. Turner," Jack tried not to flinch from his unsavoriness. "I suggest you leave my client alone from now on. The order will take effect shortly, and you don't need a violation of a court order to add to your problems, do you?"

"What the hell did I ever do to you?" Turner pointed a gold covered finger at Adam. Spitting the cigar out on the driveway, Turner yelled, "You fucking ingrate! I gave you a fucking job! I paid you more money than you deserved and this is how you thank me?"

"Look," Adam shook his head sadly, "I don't want you around here, okay? Just leave me alone."

Officer Smith announced, "Okay, Mr. Turner, time to go."

"Get your fucking hands off me. None of those fags can prove a fucking thing in court, you hear me? Let 'em try! Let 'em go in front of a damn jury and say they were fags who suck cock! Let 'em!"

Jack winced at the rolling stream of profanity and disgust coming from the fiend.

"I expected loyalty from you, Adam!" Turner waved his hands in anger. "I thought I could trust you. You think you're squeaky clean? You think that shit won't come out about you in a trial?"

"I didn't force men to suck my cock." Adam shivered in disgust.

"All right." Jack stood between them. "Enough. Please, officers, you have to get them apart. There's a trial pending."

"Let's go!" Officer Smith grabbed Turner's elbow.

"I said get your fucking hands off me!" Turner warned.

Jack stood next to Adam and watched the cops force Turner to get inside his car and leave. And seemingly wanting to have the last word, Turner opened his window and shouted to Adam, "You won't get away with this betrayal, Lewis! I'll get you for this!"

"Is that a threat, Mr. Turner?" Jack replied.

Turner just flipped them off with his middle finger and backed out of the driveway. When he sped away, the cops waited until he vanished.

"Soon there will be a court order separating them," Jack reaffirmed to the police. "Please consider driving by here on occasion."

"We will."

As the police officers left, Jack waited, feeling Adam move closer to him. Once they were alone and the area seemed strangely quiet after such turmoil, Adam whispered, "Thank you."

Facing him, Jack replied, "I can see why you're worried. He's a big man with a hot temper."

"He's a beast. A disgusting beast." Adam stared off in the direction Turner had left. "You want to come in for a minute?"

Jack nodded, following Adam inside. The interior was cool in comparison to the heat outdoors. Ceiling fans spun and the walls were white stucco. The décor had a southwestern feel that some of the southern California homes adopted. American Indian tapestries on the walls, ceramic tile floors, cactus plants, and a view of the ocean to die for.

"Great place." Jack walked to the back window and its panoramic vista of the Pacific Ocean.

"Yes. I do feel very lucky to live here. The beach is beautiful." Adam's mobile phone rang. He asked Jack, "You mind? My clients have been going insane since the gossip spread."

"No, go ahead."

"There's booze right there. Help yourself." Adam pointed to a wet bar as he answered his phone.

Jack gave the alcohol a quick glance, yet was drawn to the ocean once more. Opening the sliding door, he was instantly hit with the sound of the waves and the scent of salt water. "Wow." Jack admired the expanse of sea and sand.

"Right. Sorry about that. I had intentions of coming here and writing a group email out to all our clients just to let them know I'll still be running the business… Jack?"

"Huh? Oh, yes. I get it."

"You lost on the view?"

"Yeah. It's unbelievable. I always wanted a place right on the beach. I did look around when Mark moved out—"

"Moved out? Then you two were living together?"

"Never mind all that." Jack checked his watch, it was nearing five.

"You have to be somewhere?"

Other than his workout routine, the answer to that question was no. But Jack just didn't know if he wanted Adam to learn how lonely he was. "Ah…"

"Stay for a minute." Adam touched Jack's shoulder.

"All right." Jack allowed Adam to escort him away from the ocean scene and back inside the living room. They left the door open so they could hear the crashing waves and seagulls.

"Drink?" Adam raised up a carafe of alcohol.

"No. I'm all right." Jack relaxed on a supple leather couch and opened the button to his suit jacket.

Just as Adam had a drink in his hand and was about to join Jack on the couch, his phone rang. "Crap, it's going to be insane until this is over. I really need to hire someone. I can't do this all on my own."

"Find a temp to do some of the paperwork for you."

"It's not paperwork." Adam placed his drink on the coffee table and made himself comfortable on the couch. "It's making calls. Each one of my clients has to meet with producers, go to audition, get pampered, you know the types. They can't wipe their own butts. So, I suppose we got into the habit of doing everything for them. I don't mind. Honest. I like keeping busy and doing things for them. I just can't do it on my own. I've been asking Turner for years to hire someone else, but I know why he never did."

Jack nodded. "Because of what he was doing with the pretty boys?"

"Yes. He knew he could intimidate me. I suppose there was always the risk if he hired someone they would squeal.

22

Oh well. I don't know what good it is moaning about it now."

Jack studied him carefully while Adam sipped his drink. It did seem the more he was around Adam the more irresistible he became. The shape of Adam's jaw, the bold angles of his cheekbones, the darkness of his eyebrows, all coming together for a package that was pretty damn exceptional. If Jack could stop comparing every man he met to Mark Antonious Richfield, he might actually be attracted to someone else. And Adam was attractive to him, big time. He didn't remember the last time he felt something stir between his legs from just sitting and talking casually to another man. He was growing very hard.

"Penny for your thoughts?"

Seeing Adam's concerned expression, Jack grew angry with himself for thinking of Mark every time he was confronted with a potential date. Why rule out dozens of attractive men simply because they didn't stand up to that scrutiny. It wasn't fair.

"Nothing. So, I should get to see the judge tomorrow to sign the order. Turner will be served the paperwork. After that, he will be intimidating a witness and the courts will nail his ass."

"When do I see the DA? You know, to bargain?"

"I'm waiting for Sonja to get back to me. I'll let you know in a day or two. Meanwhile, just chill. Don't get stressed out. Go stand on that sand and get lost on the tide."

A big grin appeared on Adam's face. "You ol' romantic, you."

"Me?" Jack pressed his fingers to his chest.

"Yes, you. Under all that brawn and muscle is a heart of gold."

Jack blushed. "How the hell would you know, Mr. Lewis? You've known me for all of two days."

"I consider myself a pretty good judge of character, Jack. I knew Turner was sour the first minute I laid eyes on him. I also can see star quality in a person instantly. You?

23

Way too much heart. And I bet it's been stepped on as well. Was it by the bastard in the photo you cling to?"

The pain those words inflicted shocked Jack. Though everyone around him knew it, no one said it. Not directly. Even Jennifer hinted around him finding a new man, but she never mentioned the damage Mark Richfield did to him.

"Uh oh. Did I cross a line?" Adam put his drink down and scooted closer. "I'm sorry. Look, I can't say I've been there. I've been so damn preoccupied with this job, the closest I've come to love was a couple of one-night stands. I don't even know if I'm capable of that deep emotion. I've never allowed myself. The men I have met in this business are hit-and-run types. And though you may think badly of me by my first impression, I don't want one-night stands. I swear, I can't remember the last bout of sex I had. I work so fricken hard, I drop dead at night. I don't even jerk off I'm so tired. My cock might be dead and I wouldn't know it."

Jack smiled sadly. He thought he could relate, until now.

"But you…" Adam crawled across the couch. "You've felt real love. The kind that hurts. I envy that. I've never felt a love that can make me cry. It's a sad state, Jack. A sad fucking state. Don't they say, 'It's better to have loved and lost, than never to have loved at all', or something like that?"

"That quote is bullshit." Jack caught a scent of Adam's cologne and liked it.

"It was that bad?" Adam caressed Jack's arm. "What the hell did the bastard do to you?"

"What did he do? He fell for someone else. What the hell do you think?" Jack couldn't believe he was talking about this with Adam. Jack had never spoken about the events that led to Mark moving in with Steve to a soul.

"Someone better than you?" Adam smoothed his hand over Jack's bicep.

"Obviously."

"But…" Adam squeezed the muscle under his hand. "What am I missing here? You're gorgeous, built like a

24

fucking Adonis, sweet, funny, successful—"

"Stop." Jack held up his hand. "I can't talk about it." He rose up off the couch and looked down at Adam. "I have to go."

Standing and walking him to the door, Adam opened it for him. Before Jack left, Adam said, "If I was lucky enough to get a catch like you, I wouldn't let you out of my sight."

"Thanks, Adam. You're a decent guy underneath that hard exterior you've made for yourself. Go. Go get back to your emails."

"I've had to develop a thick skin, Jack, to survive in this game. Ah, will you call me tomorrow and let me know what's going on?"

"I will. And if Turner shows up, call the cops and don't answer the door. He should be served the papers tomorrow sometime."

"Okay."

"I'll get you a copy so you can show it to the police if they need to show up."

Adam nodded. "Jack?"

"Yes?" Jack turned back around to him. He was beginning to feel tired and he still had his workout ahead of him.

"Thanks."

"No problem." Jack waved and headed to his car, feeling more weary than usual.

As Adam closed the door, he wished he knew more about what had happened between Jack and Mark. It was killing him that whatever it was could prevent Jack from opening up to the possibility of a relationship. When the telephone rang, Adam groaned and hurried to answer it.

After Jack was changed into his workout clothes, he

found a CD to listen to while he exercised and then stretched in front of the mirrors. Seeing his large body in the reflection, Jack was proud of the way he looked. It was hard work, and without steroid-enhancing drugs, just sweat and pain. Arching his back, reaching his arms over his head, Jack gasped in surprise to see someone at his doorway for the second night in a row. "Christ, Steve!"

"Sorry. I knocked and rang the doorbell but you didn't answer. I knew you were home because the lights are on and your car is in the driveway."

"What do you want?"

"To talk."

"Does Mark know you're here?" Jack lowered the music.

"No. I grabbed the key and snuck out. Look, we have to come to some kind of understanding about this."

"Why? I don't need you to gloat."

"Jack, he was going to marry Sharon. He would have moved out anyway."

"Steve, go home. I don't need to justify anything to you. Or vice versa."

"But we both adore you. We don't want you to feel this way."

Finding his fingerless leather gloves, Jack put them on and began setting up one of the machines to work his legs. "If you feel guilty, that's not my problem. I don't interfere with you guys. I don't complain. I don't do anything. It's you two who keep coming over here. Oh, and give me back Mark's keys. I don't want you two barging in anymore."

Taking them out of his pocket, Steve said, "Mark's going to kill me for giving them back."

Jack took them and set them down on one of the machines.

Once he was positioned on a piece of equipment and raising his legs to work out his thighs, Jack moaned, "Why are you still here?"

Steve ran his hands over his hair in obvious frustration.

Throwing up his hands, Steve said, "Fine. Whatever. You want to hold a grudge, hold a fucking grudge. But remember, it's you who wants out of our lives, not the opposite."

"Go home and fuck your pretty boy. Leave me alone."

"Wow." Steve shook his head. "You really need to move on, Jack. That kind of bitterness will eat you alive. Believe me. I felt the same way after Sonja dumped me."

Jack stopped moving his legs and replied, "Oh, did you know she's found a new boyfriend? Great looking guy."

"Shut up." Steve turned and headed to the door.

After he left, Jack bit his lip in anger. He knew he needed to move on. He just didn't know how to heal the hole in his heart and allow someone else in.

Chapter Three

"Jack?"

Looking up from his paperwork, Jack noticed Sonja standing in his doorway. "Come in, Sonja."

"I've set up a meeting with the DA in regards to Adam Lewis. It's today at ten. You think you can get him there on short notice?"

"Let me call him now." Jack picked up his phone, pausing before he dialed. "Sonja, can I ask you something?"

"Sure, Jack." She moved out the chair in front of his desk and relaxed on it, crossing her long legs.

Placing the telephone back down, Jack prefaced his question by saying, "It's not work related."

"Oh?"

"It's about Steve."

"Oh." Her tone changed and she rolled her eyes. "What about him?"

"If it's too personal, just tell me to fuck off."

Sonja chuckled. "Shoot."

"Why did you break it off with him?"

Reclining back in the soft leather chair, Sonja clasped her hands together on her lap as she seemed to think deeply about that answer. "I don't know, Jack. Sometimes I do regret it. He was good fun. But we had nothing in common. After a while the conversations dried up. All we had was a physical relationship."

Cringing, he wished he hadn't asked because the last thing Jack wanted to hear was how good Steve was in bed.

"Is this about Steve and Mark?" She leaned onto the desk speaking softly, her eyes darting to the picture frame. "Jack Larsen, move on. Jennifer and I hate seeing you still pining over that conceited Brit. Let it go."

"He's not conceited."

"Stop defending him."

"Never mind. I'm sorry I brought it up. Let me call Adam." He picked the phone back up. Dialing, Jack waited, finally hearing Adam's breathless voice.

"Yeah?"

"Adam? You okay?"

"Rushed off my fricken feet. What's up?"

"Can you make a meeting with the DA today at ten?" Jack looked at his watch. It was nine.

"Yes! Are you kidding? That fast? County courthouse, right?"

"Yes. Meet me and Sonja in the lobby."

"I'll be there. Thanks for making it so quick."

"Thank Sonja. She's the one who made the arrangements."

"I'll do that."

Jack hung up and nodded. "He'll be there."

Sonja stood. "You want to grab a cup of coffee downtown on our way?"

"Yes, that sounds great."

She touched Jack's shoulder as he passed her on his way to open the door. "My treat."

"Why is everyone feeling sorry for me?" he groaned. "Christ, I'm not a little boy who can't handle life."

"We don't feel sorry for you, Jack. We just love you and want to see you happy."

"So happiness has to be tied to being a couple? A person can't be happy on their own?"

"I didn't say that."

"Never mind. Let's go." Jack buttoned his suit jacket

and allowed Sonja to walk out of the office first. He caught
Jennifer's eyes as she stood in the hallway and found that
same look of worry in them. Growing annoyed, Jack tried
not to be offended. They were all his allies and were just
trying to help.

Adam paid for parking, jogging across the busy
intersection to the district courthouse. An American flag
was whipping in the warm wind on a pole attached to the
façade. Adam dodged the preoccupied pedestrians and
entered the lobby of the massive building. Taking a look
around the crowded entrance, he immediately spotted large,
blond Jack and his sleek sexy co-council, Sonja. As he drew
close he called out, "Jack!"

Jack spun around, a serious expression on his face.

"I came as fast as I could. Traffic is a mess out there."
Adam reached out his hand to Sonja. "Thank you, Ms.
Knight for getting me an appointment so quickly."

"My pleasure, Mr. Lewis, anything I can do to be of
assistance."

"Let's go." Jack gestured to the elevators.

They crammed into the already packed space. Adam felt
overheated from his trip from the parking garage and
immediately wished he could take off his suit jacket. His
nerves had kicked in, and he had no idea what he was in for.

The elevator doors opened. Seeing Jack and Sonja
getting out, Adam followed close behind them down the
hall. Though he did nothing directly to those young men,
Adam felt guilty for what he did not do. Imagining jail, a
public flogging, or at the least a large civil payout and
bankruptcy, he couldn't feel any worse.

Their shoes echoed down the long corridor. Sonja
knocked on a door lightly. A voice shouted, "Come in."
Adam read the name on the glass front: *District Attorney
Isabella Aiden.* When the door opened, he was surprised to
see three people inside the office, having expected one.

Once they entered, Jack closed the door behind them. Several chairs had been crowded in to allow everyone access to a seat. Sonja gestured around the room for introductions.

"Mr. Lewis, this is the District Attorney, Isabella Aiden. The prosecutor on the case is Aubrey Mia, and this is Detective Elijah Blake."

Hoping his hands weren't too clammy, Adam shook each person's hand in greeting.

DA Aiden gestured to a chair. "Please, sit down, Mr. Lewis."

Adam glanced back at Jack nervously. When Jack took the chair next to him, Adam wished he could hold his hand for reassurance.

"We understand you would like to cooperate in the pending prosecution of a Mr. Jack Turner."

"Yes." Suddenly his mouth and throat went dry. Adam wished he had a bottle of water.

"We have a series of questions to ask you, Mr. Lewis," DA Aiden said, "and we'll be taping this conversation. Do you have any objections to this?"

Adam looked at Jack.

Jack replied, "Just answer honestly, Adam."

Adam said, "I have no problem with you taping this interview."

"Thank you, Mr. Lewis. Detective Blake is the individual heading the investigation pertaining to Mr. Turner's activities. I will now turn the meeting over to him and Mr. Mia, for their interview."

Adam felt so hot and sweaty he was about to die. As if Jack could sense his dread, Jack asked, "Could we get Mr. Lewis a glass of water?"

Adam wanted to kiss him, he was so grateful.

"I'll go." Sonja left the room.

The detective put a small tape recorder in front of his mouth. "On this day, the first of July, 2008, a meeting is taking place at…"

While the detective completed his preamble, Sonja returned with a glass of cold water, handing it to Adam. He thanked her and took a deep swallow, hoping it would calm his nerves.

Finally the detective asked, "State your name."

"Adam Michael Lewis."

The detective began his questions. "How long have you worked for Mr. Jack Turner?"

"Ten years."

"In what capacity?"

"As an associate. I was his partner."

"Do you know Mr. Turner on a social basis as well?"

"No. Work only." Adam held his glass of water in his hand, sipping it between questions. He felt Jack's reassuring presence behind him, and knew if he needed him, Jack was there.

"Did you suspect Mr. Turner of abusing his clients?"

Adam froze. He turned around to Jack and asked in a whisper which he knew everyone heard, "Did we request immunity from prosecution?"

"No. But I am now." Jack leaned forward. "I would like my client granted immunity from prosecution for any of the information he is about to divulge. For his cooperation in assisting in the case against Mr. Turner, I would ask the court's promise that Mr. Lewis is free from blame."

DA Aiden nodded. "So granted. Mr. Lewis has been granted immunity on this day..."

She rattled off some legal jargon that Adam barely understood. All he wanted was to get out of this alive.

"You may continue your interrogation, Detective Blake."

Jack nodded to Adam. Detective Blake repeated the question. "Did you suspect Mr. Turner of abusing his clients?"

Adam hated himself completely. "Yes."

"When did you first suspect Mr. Turner?"

"Three years after I began working for him." Adam had

to take off his suit jacket, he was roasting. As he peeled it off, he felt Jack helping him. Thanking him quietly, Adam hung it on the back of his chair.

"What did you see or hear that would lead you to believe Mr. Turner was blackmailing any of these young men?"

Adam sipped his water. "He…he said some things. Implying that if the man did him a sexual favor, he would be rewarded."

"Did you ever witness any of these incidences?"

"No. It made me sick. I left the room."

"So, you are not an eye witness to any of the allegations this victim has made."

"No."

"Did Mr. Turner ever boast of these conquests to you?"

"Yes."

"In what way? What did he say?"

Adam swallowed down the bitterness of the memories. "Things like, 'He was a pretty one', or 'Nice blow job'. Comments like that."

"Did he say those comments about the young man who has come forward in this case?"

"I…I don't know who he is. No one has told me which client it is." Adam looked back at Jack again, but Jack's face gave nothing away.

The prosecutor lifted up a folder. "Logan Naveah."

"Logan?" Adam cringed. Rubbing his forehead he sighed, "No, Mr. Turner didn't mention Logan specifically." Adam felt devastated. Logan was a lovely young man, innocent to a fault.

"And you did not witness any of these events first hand, and you cannot remember Mr. Turner boasting about Logan Naveah in particular?"

"No. Look, you have to understand Mr. Turner. He's been doing this for too long. I wish I could help you. I do. I knew he was doing it, but I did nothing about it. It made me sick. I just pretended it didn't happen. Each time he would touch one of the men in front of me, I left the room, disgusted. But I was there, and no one asked me for help. No one came to me and told me to talk to Turner about it. I would have. I would have told him enough was enough."

Silence followed.

Sonja exclaimed, "There's nothing here for Mr. Lewis to add to the case or even take the witness stand. Just hearsay."

"Yes." The prosecutor appeared upset.

Adam again looked at Jack for help. But Jack couldn't do a thing at the moment to help him. "Please, tell me what to do. I can wear a wire. Get him to confess. Let me do something."

"No."

Adam replied, "No?"

"I said no. Turner is dangerous and I don't want you near him." To the officials, Jack explained, "I have a court order preventing them from meeting. Mr. Turner has already showed up at Mr. Lewis' home to intimidate him. I don't want contact. Even to aid a police investigation."

Adam didn't understand. Didn't Jack want to see that beast behind bars?

"Is there anything else you need from Mr. Lewis?" District Attorney Aiden asked both her detective and prosecutor.

They exchanged looks. "Not at this time," Mr. Mia replied.

The detective raised the tape recorder to his mouth. "This ends the interview with Mr. Adam Lewis, time of completion, ten-thirty."

Adam heard a click. Finishing his glass of water, he sat still, completely drained.

"Let's go." Jack tapped him.

Placing his glass on the desk, Adam put his jacket back on.

Detective Blake said, "I'll be in touch, Mr. Lewis."

"Not without me present," Jack responded.

Sonja opened the office door. The three of them headed to the elevator. Adam felt so weak he needed to lie down.

When an arm wrapped around his shoulder, he looked up to see Jack's concern. "You okay?" Jack asked.

"No."

Sonja hit the elevator button. She stared at Jack as he looked back at her. Adam noticed the exchange but had no idea what they were communicating. Most likely, "Get rid of the dirty bastard."

Once they were on street level, Jack said, "I'll see you later, Sonja. Thanks."

"My pleasure. Goodbye, Mr. Lewis. I don't think you have to worry about anything anymore."

"Thank you, Ms. Knight." Adam waved as she left.

"Where's your car?"

"In that parking garage across the street. Why?" Adam needed a drink. So what if it was only ten-thirty?

Holding Adam's elbow, Jack escorted him through the traffic.

"Where is it?"

"Second floor. What are you doing, Jack? I'm all right. I'm not a fucking invalid."

"Shut up."

Growing upset at the babying, Adam pointed to his car as they came upon it and expected Jack to go on his merry way. When he walked right up to Adam's driver's side door, Adam stopped and faced him. "What are you doing? Are you going to lecture me on what a fucking asshole I am? How I was worthless to the prosecution and couldn't get Turner a fucking parking ticket let alone an assault charge?"

Jack felt sorry for Adam for all he had been through. No, he didn't go to police, but without a cooperative victim, what good would it have done? Adam wasn't the first man to work for a slimeball. Jack had his own experiences to compare it to. Defense attorneys? They were bottom-feeders, sharks. He certainly wasn't in a position to judge

Adam Lewis.

"You did nothing wrong in there."

"Why the hell didn't you let me help the police?" Adam asked, leaning back against his car.

"I don't want you near that bastard."

"Why not? Jack, I have to do something. Pandora's box is open. Let me get that fucker convicted. You think poor little Logan is going to be able to do it? One man's word against another? Come on."

Jack had a tremendous urge to kiss Adam. Why? What was it about handsome Adam Lewis that turned Jack on? He looked nothing like Mark. Nothing.

Adam stared at Jack waiting for a reply. "Jack, stop looking at me like that. I don't know what the hell's going through your head, but I can imagine."

"Bet you can't."

Moving to get into his car, Adam muttered, "Let me go. I have hundreds of fucking phone calls to make."

When Adam reached for his door handle, Jack caressed his bottom.

Stunned, Adam whipped around and gaped at Jack. "Did you just goose me?"

"Maybe."

"Why? Jack, don't play games with me right now. My head can't handle it."

Jack grabbed Adam's face in both hands and kissed him. So many thoughts were going through Jack's mind at that moment, he could fall over. It was the first passionate kiss he had enjoyed in years. The playful pecks he stole from Mark didn't add up to much. Not like this.

Adam thought his shoes had melted to the ground from the heat. Whatever he did in that office must have made a difference, because he never thought he ever had a chance in hell of touching Jack Larsen. When Jack's hot tongue entered his mouth, Adam groaned loudly. They were in a parking lot across from the courthouse! Didn't it matter? Obviously not.

Parting from the kiss, panting, hard as a rock, wanting to shove his hands down Jack's pants, Adam tried to catch his breath. "Holy shit, Larsen. That came out of nowhere."

"I know."

"Come to my place tonight." Adam glanced quickly around the area. Many people were coming and going around them.

A strange expression appeared on Jack's face. One Adam had seen before when he spoke about Mark Richfield. "Jack, for Christ's sake. Don't cock tease me. Either leave me alone or fuck me, but don't play games with me. You know what I'm going through."

"You're right." Jack replied

"I'm right how? Are you coming to my place tonight?"

"Yes."

"Good. Very good. Let me go, I have a ton of shit to get done before tonight."

"See you later." Jack smiled.

"Okay." Adam watched Jack walk away. Once he was alone, he dropped behind the steering wheel of his car and tried to calm down. Between the nervous interview and the shock of that kiss, Adam was exhausted. Knowing he had no time to rest, he turned on his cell phone to check his messages. As usual, there were plenty.

As Jack arrived back at the office, Jennifer was there waiting. "How'd it go?"

"Fine. Mr. Lewis really didn't have much to offer the prosecution. He never witnessed anything first hand."

"So? All in all, a non-starter?"

"I suppose. I think it was good he came forward and offered to cooperate."

"Will they take it any further?"

"No. They granted immunity before he began the

interview. He's done."

"Handsome man."

"Who?"

"Adam. Why don't you ask him for a date?"

"I have. And you're trouble, Mrs. Bernstein. I've heard about you." Jack pointed his finger at her.

"Moi?" She blinked her eyes innocently.

"Yes, you. Does the name David Thornton ring a bell?" Jack leaned over to his secretary. "Any calls?"

She handed him a stack of paper.

"Yes," Jennifer replied defiantly, "and may I remind you that David Thornton is now in a happy relationship."

"Oh? Are you the current Miss Match?"

"Maybe. And I think you and Adam are a perfect pair."

"Yeah, a pair of what, that's the question." Before she could respond, Jack headed to his office with his handful of memo notes, already having doubts and regrets about agreeing to go to see Adam. After he sat down, he removed the photo from his desk and hid it in a drawer. He has stared at Mark long enough.

Adam stepped out of the shower when he heard the doorbell. Thinking it was too early for Jack to be arriving, he grabbed a towel and looked out of his bedroom window. A gold Cadillac was parked in his driveway. "Oh, you have to be kidding me." Soon after, there was a thundering banging on his door. Dropping his towel, Adam hopped into a pair of jeans and grabbed his cordless phone on his way down the stairs, dialing 911. Before he connected he shouted through the door, "Get lost, Turner!"

"Open this door, you moron!"

"Hello? Yes, this is an emergency." Adam looked out of his peephole to see Turner's red face.

"You double-crosser! What's this fucking paperwork?"

Adam could see him waving something around. "Yes, there's a man at my door who isn't supposed to contact me.

There's a court order protecting me, and he's obviously got it because he's holding it."

"Adam! Open this goddamn door! What the fuck did I ever do to you, huh?"

"The police are on their way," the operator said.

"Thank you." Adam hung up. "I called the cops. You better leave or they'll arrest you."

"Open the damn door. Can't we have a civil conversation anymore? We worked together for so fucking long!"

"I don't trust you. My luck, you'll shoot me."

"I don't have a fricken gun. Open the fucking door, Adam."

Against his better judgment, Adam did. Before Turner could push back the screen door, Adam locked it. "Fine. What?"

"What the hell are these papers?"

"Didn't you read them? They are to keep you away from me."

"Why? What the hell am I going to do to you?"

"I don't know. Hurt me?"

"I'm not going to fucking hurt you. I need your help."

"You need more than my help, buddy. You need a shrink."

"Look, Adam-baby, you know this crap from Logan is just that—crap."

"I don't know that." Adam crossed his arms over his bare chest.

"The kid is just upset he didn't get anywhere with the auditions."

"Cut it out. I know you make the guys suck your cock. Don't play innocent with me."

"Consensual!"

Adam rolled his eyes. "Sure, you keep telling yourself that."

"In the ten years you've been with me has anyone complained?"

"They were scared to death! You think these young guys want anyone to know what they did to get a part? And ninety-nine percent of them weren't even gay. So you think they'll come forward and say they sucked a dick? Ruin their careers? Turner, you think I'm stupid?"

"No. No, Adam, you're not stupid. I did maybe push some kids, but most didn't mind."

Adam winced in disgust. "Oh, come on."

"No one said a thing! They never said no. So? What's the harm?"

"They knew if they said no, you wouldn't represent them. You know how much clout you have around here. Why are you pretending the guys wanted it?"

A strange look passed over Turner's face. "What if I wished they did? I know I'm an ugly fucker. Maybe I wished they wanted to."

"Now you want me to feel sorry for you?" Adam heard a siren. "Turner, leave. The cops will arrest you."

"Can I come back? Can we talk?"

"I don't know. Look, just get going."

Turner hurried to get inside his car. Right before the patrol car pulled up, he sped away. Adam unlocked the screen door and opened it, waiting for the officers to approach.

"Did he leave?"

"Yes. Look, it was okay. He didn't threaten me or anything."

"Do you have a copy of the order?"

"No. Not yet."

The two cops exchanged looks. One said, "We can't do anything without a signed order from a judge."

"Okay. Sorry to bother you."

After they gave him an annoyed glare, they left.

Adam shut the door. In need of some solitude he made his way to the beach. He inhaled the fresh sea air, trying to calm his nerves. Feeling the cool breeze after a hot day, he sat outside on the deck, trying to think, and then again, trying not to.

When Jack walked through his door, he noticed the message machine light was blinking. Thinking it might be Adam, he hit the play button.

"Hullo, He-man. Come play with us. Don't be like that. We want you to come over. Please?"

Jack erased it. Taking off his tie, he headed to his bedroom to undress and shower. He had second thoughts about going to meet Adam, and Mark's message didn't help matters. If there was one thing Jack prided himself in, it was never letting a friend down. There was no harm in going to hang out with Adam for a few hours. If he didn't feel like having sex, he wouldn't.

Showered and dressed in a pair of shorts and a cotton short-sleeved shirt, Jack grabbed his keys, wallet, and cell phone, heading out to his car. The minute he turned on his mobile phone it beeped indicating a message. As he started the ignition he put the phone to his ear. Mark again, begging.

Shutting it off, he tossed it down on the passenger seat and headed to Malibu.

Stirring a pitcher of margarita mix, Adam tasted it, placing two glasses out near a plate of salt for dipping. When the doorbell rang, he checked his face in a wall mirror. Before he opened the door he peeked out of the peephole.

"Hey." Jack entered the house holding a six-pack of beer.

"Thanks." Adam took the package from him. "I made up some margaritas. You like them?"

"Yes. I do."

"Or would you rather have a beer?"

"Save the beer." Jack tossed his keys down on the

41

kitchen counter.

"Salt?"

"No, thanks."

After putting the beer into the refrigerator, Adam poured some of the green liquid into a glass, handing it to Jack. Adam then prepared his own. "You want to sit outside on the deck? There's a nice breeze."

"Sounds good."

Adam felt coolness emanating from Jack and hoped it was just fatigue from a long day. Once they were lounging in chairs, facing the tide and some daring surfers, Adam asked, "So? How did the rest of your day go?"

"Okay. Usual shit." Jack sipped his drink. "Good one." He held up the glass.

"Great. I was hoping you liked it."

"I do. They're one of my favorites. I've just never gotten the hang of making a decent one."

"I can show you."

Jack shrugged, taking another sip.

In the strained silence that followed Adam moved grains of sand around the wooden deck with his bare feet. "You don't want to be here, do you, Jack?"

Jack looked guilty. "Why do you say that?"

"I can tell. I told you. I'm a good judge of character. And from the moment you walked in, I didn't get the feeling it was a warm meeting. Just some obligation."

"Oh, Christ, Adam, I'm sorry."

Adam set his glass down and moved his chair over so they could be side by side without a gap between them. "Jack, talk to me. What the hell's really going on?"

Finishing his drink in a gulp, Jack set the glass on the deck. "I'm an idiot, Adam. That's what's going on."

"You can't get over that guy Mark? Is that really it?"

Jack grimaced.

Touching Jack's massive forearm, Adam whispered, "Oh, baby, I don't know what I can do to help you. It's always this way for me… Helpless to do anything for anyone. It's a shitty way to feel."

"No. Don't take the damn blame for my stupidity."

Wanting to console him, Adam raised Jack's arm off the chair and kissed his hand. "Tell me what I can do? I'll do anything. You want me to talk to Mark?"

Hearing Adam say Mark's name in that context suddenly made Jack realize what a fool he had been. If he were Adam, he would have shouted, "Let it go, man! What are you, an idiot?" Instead, Adam wasn't condemning Jack for his continuing feelings for another man, unlike so many others had done. Turning in the chair so that he faced Adam, Jack reached for him again, like he had in the parking garage. When they kissed it didn't feel wrong. It didn't feel strange. It felt exciting. Fresh.

Jack opened his mouth wider, loving the sensation of their lips meeting and the tantalizing dance of their tongues. The most intense surge of pleasure rushed to his crotch. And before he knew it, he was hard and eager for more.

Adam could not get over the size of Jack's body. The weight lifting had made him huge. In all his life, Adam could not remember being with a man this big. Jack was a jungle gym to play on, an Everest to climb, and a sculpture of a hero come to life.

As Jack occupied his lips, Adam ran his hands over his rounded shoulders, his curling biceps, the width of his forearms with veins protruding like ropes of velvet. Adam felt like a child compared to Jack. His mere five foot-eleven, one hundred and eighty pound frame was dwarfed by this giant of a man.

And he loved it!

Adam wanted to rub oil all over Jack and slither on his muscles like a snake. When Adam opened his eyes, Jack was staring at him. The color of Jack's eyes reflected the sea; his hair, the sand. "Christ, Jack, I can't get over you."

Jack made some space between them, still gazing at him.

"Do…" Adam swallowed nervously. "Do you think I'm attractive, Jack?"

"Oh, yes."

"But not as pretty as—"

Jack put his finger to Adam's lips. "Forget about the Brit for five minutes. You're incredibly handsome, Adam."

"He's British? I'm competing with a limey? Oh great."

"Will you stop worrying?"

"I'll let my hair grow," Adam teased.

"You'd be a knock-out then."

"Yeah? You think so?"

"Oh, yes," Jack hissed more sensuously.

"Okay. No more haircuts. Anything else? Do you want me to talk with a British accent?"

That angered Jack.

"I'm joking!" Adam laughed, but Jack didn't join him. "Jack, come on. I was only teasing you. Don't get upset."

"I'm not looking for his replacement."

"You sure?" Adam ran his hand through Jack's blond waves.

"Yes. I've tried that. They broke the mold when they made him."

"Is he really that special?"

"You don't want to talk about him."

"You're wrong. I do. I think the key to understanding you, is understanding Mark."

"Let's go inside. Get me a refill."

Adam picked up his glass and entered the back of his house, closing the door behind them. He refreshed Jack's glass and watched him shoot it down like water. "You need to get drunk first?"

"It wouldn't hurt." Jack held out the glass again as Adam poured in the remainder.

"We got the beer you brought." Adam set the empty pitcher down.

"Take me to your room."

"My pleasure." Adam reached out for Jack's hand, escorting him up the stairs. When they entered Adam's private bedroom, Adam reclined on his bed, leaning up on his elbow to admire Jack as Jack investigated the interior.

"No photos?"

Laughing, Adam asked, "Who am I supposed to have photos of?"

"Family? Friends?"

"I'm an orphan," Adam chuckled. "Talk to me, blondie."

Jack guzzled the rest of the margarita, resting the glass on a dresser. Kicking off his shoes, he joined Adam on the bed, lying alongside him.

"You want the whole ugly story?" Jack asked.

"I want whatever you need to get off your chest."

"What a pathetic way to begin a relationship," Jack muttered.

"Oh? Are we beginning one of those?" Adam playfully stuck his tongue in his cheek.

"Shut up and let me talk."

"I'm shutting up." Adam rolled to his back so he could prop himself up on the pillows instead of his hand.

Inhaling deeply, Jack sighed. "I first met Mark in college. We played baseball at Stanford University. I hadn't had any gay experiences yet, but I knew the moment I laid eyes on him I was attracted."

"I thought he was from England?"

"He was born there. His father is American, his mother is English. He doesn't really have that much of an accent."

"Sorry, go on."

"I sniffed around him constantly, trying to get a feel for whether he'd experiment with me or not. He gave me the worst mixture of signals you can imagine. Most of the time I thought he was gay and petrified of admitting it or of his dad finding out, and the rest of the time I figured he was straight, because he'd flirt with women and talk about them."

45

Adam found the story fascinating. Not only was he learning the history of Jack's life, he was intrigued by anything with Hollywood potential.

"We eventually shared a room on campus. Drove me out of my fucking head. He strutted around naked at times, and he would kiss me as a tease, then ask me to go out on a double date with him. And I was so fricken scared if I told him I was in love with him and wanted to screw his tight butt, I'd lose him forever. It was a wicked game, but he didn't even know he was playing it."

Adam became distracted by Jack's biceps for a minute as Jack moved to get more comfortable on the bed, snapping back to refocus on his tale.

"We did everything together. After college we even moved in together. He was an architect, and we redesigned a house together. All the while he kept his distance, brought women home, and would flirt with me at the same time. Then," Jack shouted in irritation, "he gets engaged to this woman, Sharon Tice. She's some rich, spoiled brat that has a sugar daddy giving her everything she needs. Somehow she hooks Mark. He actually proposed and gave her a damn ring. I was completely amazed. Well, that was it, I thought, he's not gay."

Adam's eyes were riveted to Jack's. It seemed to Adam that Jack was lost in those painful memories.

"Then," Jack roared, "he suddenly stops the damn wedding, mid-vows! There's handsome Steve Miller standing in the back of the hall crying his name like some scene out of *The Graduate*. At first, I thought, 'Cool! Mark's finally admitted he's gay'. I knew he had to be. He's got all the signs. And he's not afraid to flaunt himself to men, believe me. He's the worst cock-tease. Metro-sexual my ass; he was full-blown homosexual. So there's Steve, the fantastic ex-LAPD macho cop, in agony over his lover. I had no idea they had been having an affair. And obviously neither did Sharon. Oh, we teased Mark about it. She suspected it more than I did because I was convinced if

Mark loved a man, it would be me. What a fucking idiot I was.

How could he not love you?

He said he did, but not in a physical way.

Adam choked at the irony, looking at Jacks incredible build. Uh, yeah, whatever.

So, hes wild about Steve, and believe me, Steve feels like he won the damn lottery. Theyre inseparable.

And? Adam inquired. So, now that Marks found his man, you cant seem to get over the fact that he did and you cant?

I did see one guy for a while. Ray. He was Sharons ex I know, it sounds incestuous all this mixing and matching. But it didnt last. In the end, he was as shallow as Sharon. I suppose thats why the two were dating.

Sounds like they were a perfect match.

Thats it in a nutshell, Adam. And here I am.

Laying on a bed with a man whose business partner is charged with sexual assault. Man, youve come a long way.

Jack began laughing. Adam was glad to see it. Jack needed a good laugh.

Okay. Your turn. Jack reached out to hold Adams hand.

Me? Im boring compared to you.

Oh, come on. All those up and coming stars knocking at your door? You must have had some fun with them.

No. No one was up or coming in my back door. I couldnt. I had so many reasons to keep my distance. Look, Jack, I knew what Turner was doing to them. You think I was going to make an advance on one of those young guys? No way.

No one? Im having a hard time believing that.

Well, one. But he wasnt a client. He was Ewan Gallaghers lover. A doctor from Carlisle, England. You know, the charming British accent, like Mark. Man, he was some piece of meat. Holy shit. I tried, he rebuffed me, life went on.

Thats it?

Jack, I dont want to rehash my sordid love life with you. I have had anal sex. Is that what you want to know? Am I a virgin?

I wouldnt care if you were.

Are you?

No. I had sex with Ray. Only him so far.

Okay, then were familiar with the art of man on man loving. Now what?

I dont know.

You want to come back in a year when my hair is down to my shoulders? Adam expected some annoyance, but to his relief, Jack laughed.

No. I dont want to wait a year. Ive already waited too damn long.

I hear ya. I swear, like Ive said, I am so busy I drop dead at night. I cant remember the last time I came.

Jack opened the top button of Adam s jeans.

Adam stared down at Jacks hands. Will you run away if its broken?

No. Ill give you a lube job and check under your hood.

Wow. You sure? I mean, after what you just told me. How the hell could I ever live up to Mark Richfields standard?

Im not asking you to. Besides, thats a question only Steve can answer.

True. Adam felt his zipper going down. Even though he was wildly attracted to Jack, he was nervous Jack was simply trying to convince himself he could have sex with someone who was not Mark. And someone more appealing than Ray, obviously. What Adam wanted to know was what did this have to do with him?

He held Jacks hands back for a moment.

It seemed to surprise Jack. I thought it was what we wanted.

When Adam Met Jack

Jack, I want it. Believe me. Theres nothing I want to do more than to get you naked and crawl around on you, you hot motherfucker. But

But?

Are you doing this to prove something to yourself, or is this for us? Us as a couple?

Jack didnt know how to answer. He assumed it was for them, as a couple. But was it?

Rolling to his back, Jack stared at the ceiling fan as it spun slowly, silently, blowing cool air on them, and tried to figure out what he was doing.

Adam adjusted his position on the bed, lying on his side. Propping his head up in his palm, Adam rested his hand on Jacks chest. Well?

I thought we were doing it for each other.

Because?

Adam! Quit the psycho-babble. If you dont want me, Ill leave.

Hang on a minute, Mr. Larsen! Adam gripped Jacks shirt and almost tore it holding him back. I want you. Hello? I thought I made that clear the first second I set eyes on you in your office. Remember my exclamation of wow? It was said because of my instant attraction for you, you fucking Adonis. So, if you think youre going to lay this one on me, pretending I dont want you, you can forget it.

Jack felt as if his head was going to burst. He wished he had someone to tell him what to do. Someone he trusted. That was insane. Everyone he trusted was telling him what to do. He just wasnt listening.

Feeling Adam move away, Jack turned over his shoulder to see what he was doing. Adam got up from the bed, he began undressing.

Waiting for those articles of clothing to drop, Jack wanted to see Adam naked, to know if he turned him on.

His face certainly did. When Adam's shirt dropped to the carpet, Jack admired his tight fit body, sparse chest hair, and a flat, washboard stomach. Looks like I'm not the only one who works out, Jack whispered.

I started after my advance on Dr. Jason Philips. The man was like you, a workout machine but not nearly as big. He made me feel guilty.

I'm glad he did.

Adam stepped out of his pants and briefs. Standing tall, he asked, Well? Suitable for a fuck?

Very suitable.

Your turn.

Standing up off the bed, Jack faced him. Unbuttoning his shirt, he dropped it, pulling down his shorts.

My, oh my, Jack Larsen, you are unbelievable.

Jack felt the blush rush to his cheeks. Not too bulked up?

What? Adam choked. What planet are you from? Get your brawny ass over here!

Moving around the bed, Jack stood in front of him.

Manhandle me! Adam laughed. Pick me up, carry me! Jesus, Jack, make me feel like your sex toy.

Unable to resist, Jack began laughing again. You are hilarious, Mr. Lewis.

I'm serious. I can't have a man like you around and not want to be dominated. Dominate me!

Okay. I get it. Jack wrapped his arms around Adam's waist and picked him up, tossing him over his shoulder. Where do you want to fuck? Pick a room.

Anywhere. Holy crap. I must feel like a feather to you.

Yup. You do. Jack slapped Adam's bottom.

Ouch! Hey, cut that out.

You want to feel dominated? Jack spanked his butt again.

Bad boy! Adam smiled. Oh, man, that gave me a hard-on.

Jack slapped him again.

When Adam Met Jack

Oh, baby! Adam could not stop laughing. Ive got rubbers and lube in the nightstand. Use them!

Jack tossed Adam roughly on the bed. Hunting down the items they needed, Jack sat down and opened a box of condoms.

While Jack was busy, Adam wrapped around his back from behind, barely getting his arms around Jacks girth. Look at your back. Holy crap, I swear I cant believe how powerful you are. Let me come on you.

Wouldnt you rather come in me? Jack held up a rubber.

No no, let me. Come on.

Do what you like. Jack shrugged.

Lay down lay down on your back. Let me come on your chest.

Setting the rubber down, Jack moved to the middle of the bed. Adam knelt up next to him, ogling his body while he masturbated. You are so amazing, Jack.

You sure you dont want me to suck it for you?

Not this time. Wait. Im almost there. Adam gazed at Jacks thighs. The size of his quadriceps was nearly the width of Adams waist. Next Adam stared at his abdomen. The eternal oblique, the wall of his stomach, perfectly cut. And lastly Jacks chest. Two huge mounds of flesh topped with tiny rose colored nipples. Ah! Adam spurted come all over Jacks skin. When he opened his eyes he found Jacks wry smile.

Its like Im looking at a damn magazine. Adam panted, trying to recover.

Thank you. What an amazing thing to say, Adam.

Are you kidding me? Adam shook his head. By all rights you should be a conceited bastard. Look at you.

My turn yet?

Wait. Wait. Adam dove on him, slithering all over Jacks hard body coating them both in semen. Oh, so niceso nice

Jack couldnt deny he loved it. The adoration, the kindness, the humor, every minute of it. Allowing Adam his wriggle session, Jack cuddled him warmly, looking for a kiss. Finding Adams mouth, he stopped Adam from moving, clutched him tightly, and sucked at his tongue and lips hungrily. Hot sex. When did he have sex this hot? With Ray? No. Not with Ray Puget. No. In his fantasies with Mark? Yes. But this was no fantasy.

Rolling Adam over gently, Jack reached for the rubber, sliding it on, then the lube. When he was prepared, he gazed down at Adam and asked, Ready?

Oh, yes. Come and get it. You want me face up, or down.

Up.

Adam nodded.

Jack raised Adams legs up to his shoulders.

Christ, Larsen, put some pillows under me. Im halfway off the bed youre so tall.

Reaching to help get Adam comfortable, Jack finally had them both ready and moved in for the connection. Visions of Mark were trying hard to get inside his brain. Little nasty voices were asking him what sex with Mark would be like. Cursing his internal dialogue for allowing his thoughts to wander, Jack forced himself to stare at Adams face as he pushed inside. This was Adam Lewis. Adam. Not Mark.

Never releasing his gaze from Adams, Jack pumped his hips in determination to get rid of that fucking ghost once and for all.

Adam could see Jacks inner battle. He knew exactly what was going on. Thats it, baby, Adam encouraged, knowing Jack was struggling to focus. Fuck me, Larsen, fuck your slave. I adore you. Take me, take me and own me.

Closing his eyes, Jack grunted a deep, masculine sound and came, clenching his teeth, showing off the large rounded muscles of his jaw.

Adam was so relieved Jack climaxed, he could weep. He had terrible images of Jack not being able to orgasm with his intruding thoughts of Mark. But he did. He came.

Pulling out gently, Jack let Adams legs rest back on the mattress

As Jack tugged off the spent rubber, Adam sat up and wrapped his arms around Jacks neck. You were fabulous.

I didnt do anything. You did it yourself. Jack asked, Is the bathroom through that door?

Yes. Adam followed him to wash up. Jack, I didnt do it myself. You let me do what I want. And thats what a good lover does. Believe me. I want you to suck my cock. Wait five minutes and you can have your wish. After wiping himself up, Adam handed back the damp washcloth.

Five minutes? Wow. I cant do that anymore.

How old are you, Jack?

Thirty-fucking-eight years old.

So? Im thirty-fucking-five. You trying to tell me thats old?

Im not twenty anymore.

Who the hell wants to be twenty? Adam took the cloth from Jack and set it near the sink. He dragged Jack back on the bed with him, curling around him. I dont want to be that age again. Im older, wiser.

I feel like I havent matured a day since college.

Stop. Quit torturing yourself Hey, you want to stay over?

Jack sat up to see the clock.

What time do you have to get up?

Ive got court at eight-thirty.

Up to you. I can get you up in time.

Set the fucking alarm.

Smiling in delight, Adam did, urging them both under

53

the blanket. Snuggling close, Adam felt like Jack was his guardian angel, his knight in shining armor. And he loved it.

It felt so good to have a man in his arms again, Jack couldn't get over the relief. Adam felt wholesome, smelled good, and said all the right things. This was what he needed. Adam.

Chapter Four

Having woken up very early in order to get home, change, and make it to court on time, Jack felt rushed. But it was worth it, he whispered. He and Adam had made tentative plans to meet up again later. The thought of it excited Jack.

Tying his tie in the bathroom mirror, Jack fixed the knot under his chin and heard his phone ringing. Knowing he was already running late, he ran to it and said, Hello?

Where were you last night, He-man?

Mark, Im on my way out the door. I cant talk.

I called you until midnight, and on your mobile.

I said, Im late. I have to be in court.

You better call me later, Jackie, or Ill be cross with you.

Gotta go. Jack hung up and grabbed his jacket and keys. What the hell do you want from me, Richfield?

Adam sat at the computer in his home, typing emails and talking on the phone simultaneously. He wore a headset, so his hands could be free. Yes, youre scheduled to meet with Orin at one. Do you need me there with you, or do you just want a driver, Roger?

Just a driver.

Good. I could go, but Im swamped.

Whats going on with Turner?

Turner? What about him? Look, I dont know a thing about it. You just dont worry and Ill take good care of you. Go see the damn director, get the script, and get back to me. He hung up, dialing another number. Yes? Rob? Its Adam, Ive got you scheduled for a hair appointment at noon, then you go directly to the photo studio for headshots.

Losing track of his typing, Adam slowed down. He felt like hed have a stroke if he didnt. Leaving the email for a moment, he concentrated on the call. Okay?

Whats going on with Turner? Do you know?

No, I dont know whats going on with Turner. Will you just get to your appointments and get back to me if you need anything else? Adam hung up, threw the headset down on his desk, and closed his eyes, trying to catch his breath. I cant keep doing this all by myself. I cant.

His cell phone rang again. Rubbing his face tiredly, he picked it up and said, Adam Lewis, here.

Adam?

Yes?

Its Logan.

Adam felt a chill rush up his spine. Logan. How are you?

You know.

Look, Im so sorry about what youre going through.

Thanks, Adam.

Is there anything I can do?

Help me. Help me find work. No one will even talk to me. Im going broke, Adam. Turner has already spread the word that Im some sort of troublemaker.

Adam had a thought. It was a long shot, but it was a thought. Uh, Logan, I know you want to act or be a model.

Yes! Thats exactly what I want.

But in the meantime? Until this blows over? Do you want some work right now?

Doing what?

56

Adam felt terrible about asking. I need help, Logan. I'm drowning here.

You need help? What kind of help?

Making appointments, scheduling meetings. You know our list of clients is enormous, and Turner handled most of the top guns. I can't seem to catch up.

I don't know how to do it.

Its no big deal. Just call people, answer calls, take messages.

Okay.

Adam blinked and sat up. Did you say okay?

Yes, but if this case goes to trial, how will it affect things? I mean, wont it look bad that Im working for the same company that I am charging with a crime?

Oh, crap. Never mind.

No, Adam, I need the work, I need the money.

But Logan, I dont want to jeopardize your court trial.

After a sad laugh, Logan replied, You actually think I have a chance in hell? My word against Jack Turners?

Let me call my attorney and get back to you.

Adam, dont. Just let me do it secretly.

Looking around his study, Adam wondered who would find out. Well, all his clients for one. No. Logan, let me just make a quick call. I have your number, right?

Let me give it to you, just in case.

Adam jotted it down. Ill call you back.

Thanks, Adam.

Disconnecting the line, Adam dialed Jacks office number.

Bernstein, Larsen, Knight and Associates, how may I direct your call?

Jack Larsen, please. This is Adam Lewis.

Hes in court right now, Mr. Lewis. Can I have him call you back?

Ill try his cell phone. Thanks. Adam hung up and dialed again. He got Jacks voicemail. After leaving a message, Adam threw down the headset again and walked to the back window to stare out at the ocean.

Its all we can do, Jack, Jennifer whispered. The rest is up to the jury.

I know . Look, were not miracle workers. Jack stepped outside the courthouse into the sunshine.

You want to grab some lunch?

Sure. Jack removed his mobile phone from his pocket and turned it on. Instantly it beeped to alert him he had messages. While he and Jennifer walked to a café, Ja listened to his voicemail. Two from Mark and one from Adam . You mind if Im ake a call?

No, dear, go right ahead. They paused at an intersection, waiting for the traffic signal to change.

Adam ?

Jennifers eyes darted to his when he said Adam s name.

Oh, thank fuck. W here are you, Jack?

I just got out of court. Whats wrong? Are you all right? Jennifer nudged him on his arm when the light changed.

Im fine. I just wanted to ask you a question. You know , now that Turner is under indictment, hes not doing anything at the m om ent with all our clients.

Yes.

Jennifer led Jack to a café.

Logan called me. Hes broke and desperate for work.

Logan? The plaintiff?

Yes. Ineed help, Jack. But would he suffer in court if I hired him ?

Yes! You cant have him work for you now . Not while you and Turner are in business together.

Can I just say hes only under my employ?

Adam

Jennifer tapped Jacks arm .

Hang on, Adam , he said, asking Jennifer, W hat?

When Adam Met Jack

Tell him to get his own business name and license. Separate from Turners. I can do it for him quickly.

Really?

Yes. Does he want it to just be in his name?

Hold on. Jack went back to the call. Adam, Jennifer is here with me and she suggested you re-open under your own name.

Can I do that? Wont Turners sue me?

Adam, do yourself a favor. Go hire a temp. Jack followed Jennifer to an open table in the café.

Okay. I get it. Thanks, Jack.

You stopping by later? Jack asked.

Yes, Ill see you at your place.

Okay. Jack hung up and noticed Jennifers concerned expression. Its a bad idea, Jen. I cant let him go that route.

Once this is done, he can file for control of the company.

Let him just start his own, and whatever clients decide to come along, will.

So? You two dating?

Yes, he answered curtly. Now, be quiet and order some food.

She smiled smugly at him and picked up the menu from the table.

It was early, but Adam didnt care. He felt so guilty about Logan, he spent all day trying to get him work. Meanwhile, a temp agency came through and was sending him a woman employee to give him a hand.

Parking his car behind Jacks, Adam climbed out and walked to the front door, ringing the doorbell. When no one answered, he checked his watch. Shit, where are you?

About take out his cell phone and call, Adam was startled by the front door opening suddenly. Widening his eyes at Jacks scant attire, Adam mumbled, Sorry, I know

Im early.

Come in. Im in the middle of my workout. Jack held open the door for him.

Mam a mia, look at you. Adam began to drool.

You mind if I finish up?

No! Be my guest. Adam closed the front door and followed Jack to a room loaded with exercise equipment. Taking off his jacket, Adam set it on a bench and leered hungrily at Jack as he gripped two barbells and continued doing curls in front of a wall of mirrors. The music of Emerson, Lake, and Palmers Pirates was on in the background. Jacks rolling biceps and bulging veins mesmerized Adam.

Relaxing next to his jacket on the leather-covered weight bench, Adam licked his lips hungrily, keeping quiet, allowing Jack the time he needed to get his routine done. Just watching Jack in action was enough to enthrall him. Who needed TV?

Loving the look of concentration on Jacks handsome face, Adam lost himself in a fantasy. What would it be like to become Jacks barbells? Be lifted in the air over his head, be used as his human-workout machine. Grinning in complete glee at that little erotic ditty, he wondered if Jack would be receptive.

Over the music, Adam caught the distinct sound of the doorbell. The dream vanished like someone had put a pin into a balloon.

Jack? Adam shouted over the noise, I hear the doorbell.

Shit. Jack grimaced.

You want me to get it?

No. Wait here. Jack set his barbells down on a rack, storming out of the room angrily.

Wait here? Adam chuckled at the absurdity. Walking to the threshold of the living room, Adam waited as Jack opened the door. Gasping in shock, Adam got his first look at the living, breathing, famous Mark Richfield.

When Adam Met Jack

Jack, this has gone on long enough! Mark shoved Jack backwards into the room. Im not letting a twenty year friendship end like this. You can forget it! You come to terms with whats going on, or Ill spank you so hard Ill wear your bottom out for weeks.

Im busy. Why the hell cant you just leave me alone? Whats with the phone calls all day? You have your life, I have mine. Jack shouted, Cant you let go of me?

I dont want to, Jackie-blue. We mean too much to each other.

Does Steve know how you feel? Is he aware how many times a day you call me?

Bollocks to Steve. Steve knows hes got me physically. He doesnt care if I call you, see you. He wants you to be part of our lives as well. Mark pointed at Adam, shouting, Who the hell is that?

Adam jumped out of his skin at the raging comment.

Jack spun around. Hes a friend of mine. Adam, this is Mark.

It all made sense now. Adam walked slowly across the room to this androgynous cat, extending his hand in friendship though he knew exactly what Mark was putting Jack through.

Mark gave Adams hand a quick shake, then crossed his arms over his chest to pout. I didnt know you had a guest. Why didnt you tell me?

Why do you need to know everything thats going on in my life? Jack countered.

Jackie, dont be that way. Mark turned his emerald green gaze back at Adam. What are you staring at, mate? Mark sneered.

The bane of Jacks existence, obviously, Adam shot back. Jack laughed.

Oh, this is bloody rich, Mark snorted. What did you tell him about me, Jackie? Hmm?

That youve become a pain in the ass and not in a good way. Jack headed back to the workout room.

Mark brushed by Adam in pursuit of Jack. Taking a good look at Mark from the back, Adam shook his head in awe. Even with all his years as a Hollywood agent, he'd never seen anyone quite like Mark.

Mark obviously was at home in the mass of workout equipment. Following them, Adam sat back down on the bench he had inhabited previously, watching these two men as if they were a study of human homosexual nature.

Standing next to Jack as he picked up his barbells to continue where he had left off, Mark curled around a chrome pole as seductively as an erotic dancer. "Why can't we be friends? I don't get it."

"We are friends, Mark," Jack said between exerting breaths. "We just don't have the same commitment to each other as we once did. Don't you get that?"

"No." Mark pouted dramatically. Adam figured it was most likely a practiced expression. "Steve and I want you to come out with us. What's so bad about that?"

"Because. The sight of you two pawing one another isn't on my list of top ten things to do." Jack set down the weights and picked up two heavier ones. "You all right there, Adam?"

"Peachy-keen, Mr. Larsen."

"Sorry about this," Jack apologized.

"Don't worry about it." Adam looked back at Mark who was giving him the evil eye.

Sauntering over, Mark asked Adam, "You two a couple or something?"

Adam wasn't intimidated by the likes of Mark Richfield. He'd had ten years of the vicious Jack Turner behind him. "Why? Jealous? Now that Jack may have a new man in his life you suddenly feel possessive?"

"What a brute!" Mark gasped. "Is he your new pit-bull, Jackie?"

"He's my new everything, Mark." Jack pulled up the weights alternatively, left, then right, as he did.

Adam loved that reply. He grinned at Mark with

superiority.

"Who are you? What do you do?" Mark drew nearer.

Adam caught a whiff of his enticing cologne. Even though Mark was a sexual icon, Adam didn't alter his expression in any way to show Mark had an effect. "Nosy fucker, aren't you?"

"Cheeky!" Mark laughed.

"What the hell is it you want from Jack anyway?" Adam asked.

Mark made himself comfortable on the bench next to Adam, leaning on Adam's shoulder. "He's practically my brother. He and I are as close as any men can be without sex. What's wrong with me wanting him as a friend?"

"Why is it about you? Have you considered Jack's feelings? Thought about what you have done to him?"

Mark gaped at Jack. "What did you tell him, He-man?"

Adam chuckled at the appropriate nickname.

"Everything." Jack finished more repetitions and set the weights down, taking a break. The music had stopped so he turned the stereo off. "Why? Don't you want people to know what you did to me? Or are you embarrassed?"

"What I did to you?" Mark blinked. "I was your best mate through college, and beyond. What the bloody hell did I do to you?"

Adam shook his head. "Are you that naïve? Man, you're like a dumb blonde."

"Oi! Watch it, mate!" Mark snarled.

"All you Brits are the same." Adam thought about Dr. Phillips, smiling at the irony.

"I was only born there, Adam. I'm a yank, just like you."

"Oh, you're nothing like me, Mark. Believe me."

"What does that mean? Jackie, is he insulting me?"

Jack didn't answer, but Adam noticed he couldn't wipe the smile off his face.

"Look," Mark began, "I'm just asking for a truce. That's all. Perhaps occasionally we can all get together for dinner. Is that so unreasonable?" Mark looked at Jack, then at

Adam. "Well?"

"It isn't up to me." Adam nodded to Jack who was doing press-ups over his head with an enormous amount of weight.

"Jackie?" Mark purred.

"Whatever."

"Good! I'll tell Steve to make reservations."

"Wait a minute," Jack interrupted. "Adam and I are really busy at the moment."

"Busy doing what?"

Adam shook his head. "Nosy, nosy…"

"Oh, shut up," Mark quipped. "Tell me when, then, Jackie."

"How many times have I said, I'll call you?"

"Too many. And you never do!" Mark leaned harder against Adam's shoulder. "He never calls."

"Do you blame him?"

"Yes! Stop defending him. Are you a lawyer, too?"

Adam had to laugh; it was all so damn funny.

Setting down the weights, Jack walked directly in front of Mark and enunciated loudly, "I'll call you."

"Did you understand that?" Adam teased. "Or do you need it translated into blonde bimbo?"

"Oi! You are a cheeky-monkey!" Mark replied, laughing. "I like him, Jackie. Where did you find him?"

"In my office, like you found your ex-LAPD cop."

"Oh, I see. The plot thickens."

"Mark, I have to get in the shower, and Adam and I have plans."

"Is that a hint for me to leave?"

Unable to resist, Adam added, very slowly and clearly, "Yes, it means you need to leave now."

"Don't push it." Mark winked. "Okay, chaps, I'm out of here." He rose up off the bench.

Adam followed them to the front door.

"Don't make me wait too long, Jack. I'll give you a week, then I'll come hunting again."

"Will you stop putting time limits on me?" Jack asked.

"No. Never. Goodbye, cheeky-monkey." Mark waved at Adam.

"Goodbye, Mr. Richfield."

After Mark had left, Adam stared at Jack for a moment until Jack said, "See what I mean?"

Letting out a blast of air, Adam said, "Christ, Jack, he's sex on a stick."

"I know. Come on. I need a shower."

Adam followed happily, wondering what it would be like to hang out with Jack, Mark, and his ex-cop lover. How bad could that be?

Jack was smiling as he headed to his bedroom with Adam close behind. It felt good. Adam seemed to handle himself well and never indicated he was captured by Mark's allure. As he entered his room, Jack suddenly realized he had a few framed photos on display of him and Mark. Before he could apologize to Adam for it, he noticed Adam had already picked one up to inspect.

When Adam held it out for Jack to see, Jack said, "That was when we were both on the ball team in college. Mark was selected MVP."

Adam replied, "You know, it doesn't help that his image is everywhere."

After kicking off his tennis shoes and socks, Jack pulled his tank top over his head. "No. It doesn't. And I'm going to get rid of them now."

"Don't do it on my account." Adam set it back down on the dresser.

"No, it's for me." Jack couldn't wait. He walked across the room, stacked the few frames, placing them in his closet and closed the door. "That was easy."

"Yes. It was."

Heading into the bathroom, Jack removed his gym shorts and briefs, intent on a hot shower. He felt a hand on his bottom. Jack smiled. "Yes?"

"I loved watching you work out."

"You can come by anytime. I do it every day but Sunday. Monday through Friday after I come home from work, and Saturday mornings. If you'd like, you can bring your gear and join me."

"I notice you have a treadmill."

"It's all yours." Jack remembered Mark used to run on it while he lifted weights. "It's nice to have the company."

"Thank you, Jack. I'll take you up on that."

"Let me rinse. I'm a sweaty mess." Jack pushed back the sliding door and turned the water on.

"Believe me, I'm not offended by your sweat."

Grinning at him, Jack stepped into the crashing water and washed. He noticed Adam leaning against the wall, staring at him.

"So, ah…what do you think about Mark?"

"He's all right. I think he's a little insecure. All that pomp and circumstance is hiding a scared little boy."

"Man, you're good. That's Mark all over." Jack shampooed his hair, closing his eyes. After he rinsed out the soap, he opened them to see Adam, naked, climbing in. "Hello!" Jack laughed.

"Sorry. If you think I can stand there and watch without getting in with you, you're insane. Give me the damn soap."

Giving out a hearty laugh, Jack handed him the bottle, knowing the closer he and Adam became, the less Mark Richfield seemed to matter.

Adam blobbed some coconut scented soap in his hand and began washing Jack's chest. It was swollen and hard from his workout. Instantly Adam's body responded. His sole concentration was on Jack's taut skin over those protruding pectorals. Adam smoothed one hand on each rounded mound in a circular motion that hypnotized him. He was completely lost on the size of Jack's chest when

66

Jack's hands gripped Adam's cock. Adam was already struggling to keep his eyes open as the urge to climax crept up on him quickly. His palms brushed over Jack's erect nipples while Jack's soapy fingers worked his cock like he was climbing a rope, hand over fist. Clenching his teeth, he came, holding onto Jack for balance.

After the swoon, Adam blinked as if coming awake. Slowly, he crouched down in front of Jack, the hot water cascading over their bodies. At eye level with that lovely dark blond pubic hair, Adam opened his lips and drew Jack's hard cock into his mouth. Hearing Jack's moan, feeling him reach back for the tiled wall, Adam relished the desire to please him. Gripped to Jack's thighs, Adam allowed Jack's length to pump in and out of him. Jack was fucking his mouth, thrusting his hips deeply into Adam. When Adam felt Jack was nearing the peak, he wrapped his hands around the base of Jack's cock and gripped it tight. A few quick thrusts and Adam tasted come. Allowing it to run down his throat, Adam felt high from it. He was tired of being alone. Worn out from the plastic Hollywood-types that were selfish to the core, he had to admit he adored this kind-hearted man. Adored him.

Jack slowly recovered. Shutting off the faucets, they both stood, dripping silently. Sliding back one of the doors, Jack reached for a towel and handed it to Adam, taking another one to rub on his own face and body. After Adam stepped out of the tub, over his pile of clothing, Jack caught his eye, giving him a generous smile.

Adam returned it. Hanging up the towel over the shower door, Adam picked up his clothing and asked, "Are we still going out to dinner?"

"Anything you want." Jack climbed out of the tub, finished drying, and waited for a reply.

"Are you hungry?"

"A little."

"It's early. Only just past six-thirty. Want to cuddle in bed for a little while?"

"Sure." Jack followed him into the bedroom, turning off the bathroom light.

Once Adam set his clothing down on a chair, he turned down the bed and crawled under the blankets. Jack snuggled with him, squirming under the cool crisp sheets. Finding Adam's mouth, Jack kissed him, leisurely, licking him as if he were a chocolate candy. Minutes passed, the kissing became more of a session in loving with just their lips and tongue. Jack couldn't remember doing this with anyone else. The way Adam kissed him was so sensual, so enticing, Jack wanted to do it all night.

Finally, after a satisfying bout, Adam stared into Jack's eyes. "I'm really enjoying our time together, Jack."

"So am I, Adam." Jack pushed Adam's damp hair away from his forehead.

"I hope we can continue to see one another."

"Me, too." Jack smiled. "Why can't we? You going somewhere?"

"No. I have nowhere to go."

"Good."

"Hungry yet?"

"Yes, how about you?"

"Starved." Adam kissed Jack's cheek.

"Okay, let's go grab a bite. We have all night to get back in bed."

"We do indeed!" Adam rolled on top of Jack and pressed his hips against his.

"What are you in the mood for?"

"Anything. I'm not picky." Adam licked Jack's chin playfully.

"I know a great Italian restaurant. Best pizza around," Jack suggested.

"Sounds fantastic."

Pulling Adam closer for one last, good kiss, Jack moaned in pleasure, the thought of Mark never crossed his mind.

Chapter Five

"Natalie," Adam said, "I want you to answer this phone. When clients call, write down what they need and then make a list for me. Eventually, I'll give you all my contacts. From then on all you need to do is make appointments for them, call them back, and check the time you have arranged is good. Okay? That's really it."

"Okay, Mr. Lewis."

"Adam, call me Adam." The phone rang. Adam nodded to it. They were in his home office far away from Turner's posh Hollywood set-up. Natalie was sitting at Adam's desk and he stood behind her. She picked up the phone. "Hello, Turner and Lewis Agency, how can I help you? Who? Logan Naveah?"

Adam tapped her shoulder. "Let me take this one."

She nodded, handing Adam the phone.

Walking out of the room with it, Adam said, "Logan, listen, I've got you an audition. It's with a very good friend of mine."

"Does he know what's going on?"

"He does. And he can't stand Turner, so don't worry. Just do your best."

"Great! Give me the address and time."

Adam scrambled to get out his electronic notebook, scrolling through the information stored in it. "Got a pen?" After he gave Logan everything he needed, Adam wished him, "Good luck." Handing Natalie back the phone, he said, "Sorry about that. That one was a special case."

"Okay."

"Check the voicemail to see if anyone left messages." He showed her how to do it.

"Okay." She began jotting down the information on a pad. Adam was relieved she was picking it up quickly. It immediately took a load off of him.

Jack sat in the conference room for their office briefing. Jennifer led the meeting as each attorney went around the room explaining where they were on their current cases, as well as being assigned new ones. Sipping a cup of coffee, Jack relived last night, humping Adam happily, dripping with sweat as if he'd just run laps.

"Jack?"

"Hmm?"

"Anything you'd like to add?"

"Uh, no."

Smiling at him, Jennifer observed, "You look lost in thought. Anything you want to share with the group?"

"Definitely not!" he laughed.

"Uh huh, well, on that note, meeting adjourned."

As the group disbanded, Sonja drew closer to Jack. "Anything going on with Turner's case? Has the DA contacted you again to call Adam as a witness?"

"You know, Sonja, I'm not convinced that thing is even going to make it to trial."

"You may be right. Keep me in the loop if you hear anything."

"I will."

Jack headed to his office, taking his cell phone out of his pocket. When it connected, he purred, "Hello, baby."

"Hi, lover."

"How's your day going?"

"Great. The agency sent me a temp, and she's very

efficient. I don't feel like I'm drowning anymore."

"I'm very glad to hear that. Still coming by to work out with me later?"

"Can't wait."

"Good, see ya then." Jack hung up and pocketed his phone, whistling on his way to his desk.

Adam watched Natalie take calls and write up requests. Hearing his doorbell, Adam excused himself from her and hopped down the stairs with a light, bouncy gait. Opening the door, his smile dropped at the sight of the dreaded Mr. Turner. "What do you want?"

"You said I could come by to talk? Remember?"

Adam couldn't recall if he did. "What's there to talk about?"

"Let me in. I won't bite."

"That's not what I heard."

"Fer cryin' out loud, Adam." Turner made a show of lifting his shirt and spinning around. "I'm unarmed! Okay?"

"Toss that rancid cigar out. I don't need that smell in my house."

Turner flicked it away, rubbing his hand over his jet black goatee as if getting spittle off it.

Reluctantly, Adam opened the door.

Stinking of cigars and overpowering cologne, Turner entered the room and looked around. "Who's here?"

"I hired a temp."

"What for?"

"Come on, you think I can run the damn business on my own?"

"You're not on your own. I'm here. You don't even come to the damn downtown office anymore."

"The DA won't let you conduct business until this is settled. Isn't that right?"

"Fuck the DA. Who do you need me to call?"

"Just go sit down in the living room, will ya?" Adam

was already losing his patience.

"Ya got anything to drink around here?"

"What do you want?"

"Adam?" Natalie called.

"Go help yourself, I'll be right back." Adam jogged up the stairs. "What's up?"

"Ron Juniper asked for a hair appointment for today. Where's that list of phone numbers you said you were going to give me."

"Oh. Hang on." He found his personal telephone book where he had written all his notes. "Here. You're doing great, Natalie."

"Thanks, Adam."

"Uh, I have someone downstairs. Are you okay by yourself?"

"So far. I'll just call you if I need you."

"Good. Also, as you make appointments, could you enter them on this computer screen so I can keep track?" He brought up a calendar on the computer.

"Sure."

"Thanks." He hurried back down to the first floor and found Turner mixing martinis in the kitchen. "You really don't get how serious these allegations are, do you?"

Turner handed Adam a glass, a toothpick with a green olive sticking out of it. "And you don't get how petty they are."

Sighing, placing the drink he did not want down on the kitchen counter, Adam followed Turner back into the living room. "Petty? Come on."

After he dropped his girth down on a couch, Turner sipped his cocktail casually. "It ain't the first time, Adam-baby."

Sitting down across from him, Adam folded his hands on his lap. "Go on."

"First year I was in business, two decades before you came along, some fag pointed the finger at me. Went nowhere."

"When was that?"

"I don't know, nineteen eighty-something. You were a mere sprout back then."

"Why did it go nowhere?"

"His word against mine. Don't you get it?"

Reclining on the couch, Adam rubbed his forehead tiredly. "It's you that doesn't get it."

"Adam, I'm trying to tell ya, it's business as usual. It'll blow over the moment the charges are dropped. It's just the first time you've had to deal with it. That's why you're overreacting."

"Overreacting? You're missing the whole point. Don't you get that the idea that having these guys suck your cock for a part is wrong?"

"No. *Quid pro quo*. Nothin' wrong with that. It's business."

"No. It's nasty and it's wrong."

"Now ya tell me? For ten years you've been my assistant and suddenly you're Mother fucking Theresa? Come on, Adam. Ain't you done it yourself?"

"No!" Adam shouted in horror.

"Why the hell not? You know how many pretty boys we got as clients? You're the one who's got it wrong."

"How on earth do I argue with your skewed logic?"

"Oh, come on. You had a hard-on for that English fella, what's his name. Ewan's sugar daddy."

"Yes? And? I made an advance on him. I tried to kiss him on the beach. He didn't want me to. That was it."

"That was it? You see your mistake now? All you had to do was threaten to get Ewan dropped from the agency, and that guy would have been on his knees in front of you."

Adam groaned in agony. "Man, you really need to see someone. You're sense of right and wrong is all messed up."

Pointing his gold-covered finger at him, Turner yelled, "Don't you go tellin' me right from wrong, Lewis! You're as slimy as they come. You're no different than me."

"Oh, come on! I've never made one of these young men perform sex on me for a job. How the hell do you compare us?"

"You did nothing about it. You fucking knew. What did you do? Huh? You walked away. Okay, maybe ya didn't get turned on by watchin' me do it like some guys would."

Adam cringed in disgust.

"But ya did nothin'. There I was, in my office with Ewan-fricken-Gallagher givin' me head, and you right on the other side of the damn door. You knew it. What did ya do? Don't go acting like you're some fucking angel."

"Look," Adam sighed tiredly, "we can't work together any longer."

"What? Oh, quit acting like a fucking baby. I'm tellin' ya, this Logan, he's going to get nowhere. He's a fricken foreigner to boot. Probably an illegal. He ain't got no rights in this place. Give it a month, and we'll get back to our usual."

"No." Adam stood up. "No, I'm not going to work with you. Not after this."

Fury came quickly to the big man. Turner set his empty martini glass down with a crash on the side table and rose up. "You don't make the decisions in this business, I do!"

"I'm not working with you anymore," Adam insisted.

"Then you'll be through in this town. Through! I'll take my clients and you'll be left with nothin'."

"Your clients?" Adam laughed sadly. "Do you know your clients don't want anything to do with you at the moment?"

"What have you been tellin' them ya little snake?"

As Turner advanced menacingly, Adam backed up. "Me? I don't have to tell them a fucking thing. You don't think there's gossip in Hollywood? How long have you been in this business?"

"If it's just gossip, I ain't got nothin' to worry about. If you've been verifying that gossip, that's a different story."

"I haven't. I've been telling them I don't know what's

going on."

"You better have, ya bastard."

"Or?" Adam stopped backing up. "What are you intending on doing? Aren't you in enough trouble as it is?"

"You think this is trouble? You ain't seen trouble."

"Adam? Mr. Lewis?"

Remembering they weren't alone in the house, Adam shouted, "Be there in a minute, Natalie."

"You're lucky you got a little girl in the house," Turner sneered.

"You know, just you being near me is a violation of a court order."

"Oh, go fuck yourself, you asshole. You let me the fuck in. You see? Consensual! Everyone lets me do shit, and I get the fucking blame."

"Time to go."

"You don't order me around, Adam. You never tell me what to do."

"I'm telling you now. Go." Adam pointed to the door.

"What are ya gonna do? Call the freakin' cops on me?"

"If I have to."

"You know how much I can do to you before those assholes even show up?"

Adam did. He'd been intimidated by him for so long, it was hard to act strong. "Just leave."

Moving as close as he could without touching, Turner growled into Adam's face. "I made you; I can unmake you. You watch your ass, Lewis, or you'll find yourself dead or penniless. Your choice."

Laughing nervously, Adam asked, "Are you threatening to kill me?"

"Depends how much you piss me off."

"Christ, Turner, you just keep digging yourself deeper and deeper into your hole."

"It ain't my hole I'll be digging."

Stepping back so he didn't have to inhale Turner's nasty breath, Adam replied, "You know something? After the last visit you showed some signs of remorse. You even made a comment about how you wished the boys would like you."

"Shut the fuck up."

"No. I won't. Ironically, you think it's because you're not great looking. But the real reason is the toxic waste that comes out of your mouth. If you had a heart of gold, men would flock towards you."

Unexpectedly Turner grabbed Adam by the throat, choking him. "I don't need none of your fucking opinions about my life, you got that? And if you want to keep breathing, you keep your nose out."

Shoving back from him, Adam rubbed his neck from the pain. "Get the fuck out of my goddamn house," Adam growled.

"Our partnership is done! You hear me? Don't you come crawling back when you're broke."

"Get out!" Adam opened his front door.

"And if I find out you've been talkin' about me behind my back with my clients, I'll be back, don't you worry."

"Out!" Adam couldn't shout any louder. Natalie finally appeared at the stairs to see what was going on.

Turner shoved the screen door opened so hard it clattered against the house. Once he was out, Adam shut the door, locking it.

"You okay?"

"No." Adam walked with shaking legs to sit down in the living room.

"You want me to get you a glass of water?"

"Yes, please." He dropped onto the sofa, staring at the empty martini glass and thinking about the not so empty threats.

Jack changed out of his suit and into his shorts and tank top for his workout. Checking the time, he expected Adam early for their exercise session. He remembered the ones he shared with Mark. He assumed Adam would do mostly aerobic workouts, like the treadmill and bike. Grabbing two bottles water and a couple of towels, Jack made his way to his home gym and set the things down. He picked out a CD to play after Adam arrived. Stretching side to side, then reaching down to his toes, Jack began warming up anticipating that at any moment the doorbell would ring.

Staring in the bathroom mirror at the scratches on his neck, Adam fretted at Jack noticing them. Checking his watch, wondering if he should try to cover them up somehow, Adam threw up his hands in defeat. He picked up the canvas bag and left the house.

Jack finally heard the doorbell while loading up the bar for his bench-presses. Jogging to the front door, he opened it and smiled, "You're late, Mr. Lewis!"

"Sorry."

As Adam entered his home, Jack's smile faded quickly. "What happened?"

"Nothing. Where should I change?"

Jack gripped Adam's arm to stop him from moving. "Adam, what the hell's going on?"

"I don't want to talk about it right now. I just want to get my stupid workout stuff on and run until I drop, okay?"

Having felt that way many times himself, Jack released Adam's arm. "Just change in my bedroom."

Without a word, Adam left.

Jack walked slowly to the gym, his mind jumping to all sorts of conclusions. Knowing the most obvious one, Jack grew angry as he waited for Adam to return. He started the music, keeping it low.

Ten minutes later, Adam stepped into the room wearing a pair of dark blue gym shorts and a white running t-shirt. Jack kept an eye on him from the mirror's reflection as Adam stood on the treadmill feeding the digital console his information.

"The music all right?" Jack asked, trying not to be aggressive about finding out what was wrong.

"Yes, fine."

"I can change it."

"No. I like it. It's fine."

Crosby, Stills, and Nash crooned "Dark Star" over the noise of the treadmill as it started up. Lying down on the bench, the two-hundred and fifty pound bar over his head, Jack relaxed before his exertion glimpsing over at Adam's preoccupied face.

Getting his mind back on his task, Jack gripped the bar, arched his back, and blew out a blast of air as he hefted it up. Fifteen repetitions later, he placed it on its mounts, sat up, caught his breath, and stared at Adam.

Adam had gotten the speed up quickly and was soon sprinting on the rubber mat. The noise of the whirling machine and Adam's deep gasps soon blocked out the music. Before Jack loaded his bar with more weights, he cranked the stereo up louder so it could be heard.

A half hour later, Adam slowed down the speed of his pace, catching his breath and wiping his face with a towel. Jack had moved on to do some flies with barbells on an incline board, trying not to be distracted by Adam's expression, which hadn't changed since he arrived.

Wiping down the machine with the towel, Adam stepped off, lay down on a mat, and began doing crunches, still quiet, preoccupied, and driving Jack insane.

Hating the silence, especially now that the CD had finished and the room had taken on an echoing quality, Jack set the weights on the floor. He crossed the room, and knelt down to hold Adam's feet in place while he did his sit-ups.

"You don't have to do that."

"I want to. I can stare at your crotch from here."

Adam chuckled between his crunches.

"Be better if you were wearing a jock-strap or, better yet, nothing under those shorts."

"It would chafe like hell. But for you, anything." Adam stopped, resting on his elbows, catching his breath.

"What are those scratches on your neck?" Jack leaned closer.

"Nothing." Adam did another twenty sit-ups. Jack continued holding his feet to the floor.

"Nothing? Bullshit." As soon as Adam finished, Jack crawled closer to inspect them. Then it dawned on him. "Turner did it."

"I said forget it." Adam made a move to get up.

Jack grabbed him tight, holding him still. "I won't forget shit! Adam, what the hell happened? Did you call the police?"

"No!" Adam shouted, then covered his face.

Wrestling to get Adam into his arms, Jack forced Adam into an embrace and squeezed him to his chest

I'm a big boy! I don't need anyone's help! But Adam did, very much. Battling with his emotions, not wanting to shed a tear over that fiend, he bit his lip and gripped onto Jack with all his might.

"Okay, baby. Take your time," Jack cooed, rubbing Adam's back.

When Adam felt more in control, he released the death hold he had on Jack and put some space between them. Meeting Jack's crystal blue eyes, Adam knew he could tell this man anything and he'd be supported.

Before Adam could say another word, Jack raised Adam's jaw up, looking at the marks on his throat. "He tried to strangle you."

"Yes. To scare me. Not to kill me."

"When?"

"Look, I didn't mention it, but he came by two days ago. I didn't let him in. He had just been served the court papers and was waving them around." Adam avoided Jack's expression, knowing he had withheld that information from him. "I called 911 and told him to leave. Through my locked screen door we talked for only a minute. Turner said some things, you know, like he knew he was wrong, he wished he was better looking and didn't have to coerce men, blah, blah, and I bought it."

"And?"

"Well, he asked me if he could come back, just to talk. I did feel a little sorry for the guy." He peered up at Jack and imagined Jack calling him a sucker in his head. "Uh, anyway, he left before the cops came. Then he came back today. Natalie, my new assistant was in my study, so I did let Turner in. I figured I could always yell at her to call the cops. And before Turner came in he showed me he was unarmed."

Jack's face tightened in rage.

Adam flinched but kept going. "I've known Turner for ten years, Jack. He's never threatened me, ever."

"He has a reason now."

"I know. Let me just get this out." Adam tried to stand up. Jack helped him to his feet and they both sat more comfortably on a bench. "We talked about the business. Turner was going on about when this all blows over we can get back to work. I told him I'm not working for him anymore. We got into a debate about the clients. It represents a lot of money, Jack." Adam felt confident Jack was taking in every word. "So, Turner begins accusing me of slandering him to them, of stealing them behind his back, the usual stuff someone as paranoid and moronic as Turner would say. I told him they didn't need to hear what was going on from me. That they gossip between each other. Christ, I always say I don't know what's going on when they ask. He didn't believe me. He just got carried away and choked me. He's got this vision of losing everything, just like I do. We worked very hard to be where we are, Jack, and both Turner and I don't want to lose it."

"You didn't make anyone suck your cock for a job, Adam."

81

"I know that. But Turner's convinced it's business as usual. For some reason he just cannot see anything wrong in what he did. Which was a direct turnaround from the last visit where he did admit he had fucked up."

Jack rose up off the bench.

"Where are you going?"

"I'm reporting it as a violation of a court order."

"Jack!" Adam raced after him. "I let him in. Don't. In court it'll be the same debate of who allowed what and a waste of everyone's time."

"Did he threaten you?"

Adam bit his lip. He could see the fury in Jack's eyes.

When Jack turned away again, Adam gripped him tight, but it was like holding onto a Brahma bull that had broken its pen. "Jack, don't call the cops. Please."

Halting his progress, Jack spun around and asked, "How did he threaten you?"

"I'll tell you only if you don't call the police." Adam held Jack's hand.

Jack shifted his weight side to side in what Adam figured was frustration.

"He just said if I tried to steal his clients he'd kill me."

Jack tore out of Adam's grip and picked up the phone.

"Jack! You promised."

"I fucking did not!"

"I let him in! Hello? I let him in my house willingly."

"Yes, but he is aware he has the court order prohibiting him from contacting you. He was served papers. Just driving into your driveway is a violation. And threats to kill? It's a felony, Adam."

"You get him picked up for that, and he will kill me."

Jack set the phone down.

"Thank you. I know you think I'm just a ninety-pound weakling, but I can handle Turner. I've been dealing with him for ten years."

"I don't think you're a weakling, Adam. So stop the bullshit. It's just that Turner is a maniac."

"Yes. And what do you do with a maniac? You don't antagonize him." Adam clasped Jack's hand and brought him back into the workout room. "Now, finish your routine."

"I am finished."

Adam smiled at his frown, wanting to change the negative emotions that were now plaguing them. "No, you're not. You have one more exercise."

"I do?" Jack appeared confused as if he were still preoccupied with Adam's confession.

"Yes." Adam escorted Jack to the bench-press equipment. "I want you to lift me."

Jack threw up his hands. "Okay." Jack wrapped around his waist and picked him up.

"No. I mean like a barbell." Adam wanted them to feel relief from the pressure they were under. He hoped it worked because the look on Jack's face earlier was very upsetting.

Jack set Adam down on his feet again. "Like a barbell?"

"Yes. Humor me, will you? I want us to forget this crap with Turner and lighten up. Okay? So do as I say. Lie down."

"I get it." A slight grin cracked Jack's somber face.

Adam was very glad to see it. "Good. Smile. Forget everything else and let's just play."

"Okay. I'm game." First Jack removed the empty bar from the mounts, setting it on the floor. After he lay back on the bench, he asked, "Now what?"

"Bench-press me."

"You'll topple off and hurt yourself."

"I'll take my chances."

"Let's do it on my bed."

"We'll do it there next, before sex. I want to do it in here, now."

Grinning in amusement, Jack said, "Okay, get over here and stay rigid."

"I'm already rigid, cutie." Adam was very relieved to see

83

his mood improving.

"If I laugh I won't be able to do this."

"I won't make you laugh." Adam stiffened up, slowly leaning against Jack's hands as Jack held them up. Once Jack had a good grip of Adam's leg and shoulder, he arranged Adam across his chest like a bar. "Ready?"

Adam tensed up. "Go."

Jack lifted him over his head effortlessly, doing five presses with him until Adam began laughing and his tight body collapsed into a heap on top of Jack's.

They both went hysterical laughing over it. They needed to release the tension and fear they had felt a moment before.

Adam knelt on the floor next to Jack leaning over his broad chest. "You are awesome."

"And you need to stay somewhere safe."

"No. Don't rush us. Not for that reason."

"Adam…" Jack chided.

Putting his finger to Jack's lips, Adam silenced him. Adam replaced his finger with his mouth and kissed Jack.

It was Adam's turn to pick out a restaurant. He had a favorite Mexican that, ironically, was one of Jack's first choices as well. Sitting out on the sun-drenched deck, an umbrella shading them from the scorching July heat, Adam sipped his margarita while they waited for their tortilla chips with salsa and avocado dip appetizer.

Jack kept peering over his shoulder to the parking area and the line that had formed to get inside the eatery. "What are you looking for?" Adam asked.

"Mark loves this place. I remember one evening when we were here together we bumped into Sharon and one of her girlfriends, Candice. He does come here often so be on the look out."

"So? So what if he shows up?"

"He'll want to join us."

Adam set his glass down and leaned on his elbow to gaze at Jack. "Stop being so paranoid. If he shows, we'll deal with it."

"Please don't get a crush on him."

Adam sat back, blinking in surprise. "A crush on him? Oh come on, Jack, give me some credit."

Jack leaned over to speak privately. "Everyone that meets him wants to get into his pants. Why should you be any different?"

"Because I've been around pretty boys my whole career. He's just another body. Why is it you think you can't compete with him? Do you have any idea what kind of man you are, Jack?"

"A loser who can't get what he wants?"

"Ouch."

Jack grabbed Adam's hand and squeezed it. "Sorry. Old habits. You're right. If he shows, he shows."

"Exactly. I don't want to get into Richfield's pants, just yours."

"I hope so."

Adam was having a difficult time believing Jack's doubts. Mark was nice looking, yes, but Adam didn't feel the attraction Jack suspected he would. "Order another drink. I'm driving."

"Thanks, you're a doll." Jack winked at him and as the waiter set down their appetizers, Jack ordered another beer.

Munching a tortilla chip loaded with guacamole, Adam finished chewing first before he asked, "Has Mark ever modeled?"

"He did a little. Fresh out of college a woman used him in a collection of male nudes she was doing for a coffee table book. It was called, 'Male-Men', or something like that. He had two shots in it. One naked on a white stallion, and the other in a bed with the sheets pulled down almost to a point of obscenity."

"Why didn't he pursue it as a career?" Adam kept eating. The waiter returned and set Jack's fresh beer down, taking his empty.

After the waiter left, Jack shrugged. "I don't know. I think he had architecture on the brain."

"Is that what he does now?"

"No. He's in advertising. He and Steve work for a firm called Parsons and Company."

"I bet you have a copy of that book."

"Two. Stop being so smart."

"Do you get yourself off over the photos?" Adam smiled.

"I said shut up." Jack winked at him.

"Christ, I wish I could make you that hot."

Jack gripped his hand again. "You do. Let's stop talking about him. It's not good for us, and there's no reason for it."

"You're half right. It's not good for us, but there sure as hell is a reason for it."

"No. Enough. Tell me more about yourself. Were you born in California?"

"No. Canada."

"Another foreigner? How do I find you guys?"

"Foreign? Canada? Christ, it's just Vancouver, not some French province." Adam ate another chip and shook his head.

"How'd you end up down here?"

"Dad. He was moved to LA on business. Mom didn't mind. I have a sister here as well, but we don't really speak much. I'm sort of at odds with everyone family-wise."

"Why?"

"They think I'm a Hollywood slimeball. And they're right."

"Oh, shut up, will you?"

"Where are your parents?"

"Florida. They retired there."

"I'm surprised they didn't head to Palm Springs."

"No, they were East Coasters. They're from New York originally. I came out this way for college, then followed Mark when he got a job offer down here."

"Gotcha."

The waiter arrived with their main courses. Jack and Adam made room on the table for the plates.

"Another beer?" the waiter asked.

"Yes, thank you." Jack smiled at him.

Adam waited for him to leave. "So? It takes a six-pack to even give you a head buzz?"

"Not quite." Jack set his empty glass down and began devouring his meal. "Damn, they cook good food here."

"They do. I love this place."

As they relaxed and ate their dinner, Adam heard a faint voice over the distant traffic noise out in front of the restaurant. "Oh, Jackie-blue!"

Both Adam and Jack stopped eating and stared at each other.

"You have to be kidding me," Adam muttered.

"I fucking knew it."

"Jack, don't make a big deal out of it."

Jack spun around. Mark was waving at him. An incredibly good looking man stood next to Mark. Adam assumed it had to be ex-LAPD cop, Steve Miller.

"Can we join you?" Mark asked over the heads of several people. "The wait is over a half hour."

Jack cringed; Adam grabbed his leg and squeezed it. "Up to you, babe. I don't care either way."

"If I don't, I'll never hear the end of it."

"It's okay, Jack. Trust me. I only have eyes for you."

Jack took a good look into Adam's face checking his sincerity. Adam knew Jack was sick of the competition. "Fine," Jack grumbled and waved to Mark over the top of the crowd.

Mark pushed his way past the line, dragging Steve behind him.

A waiter started making room for the two new diners at their table, placing settings down and asking what they wanted to drink.

Steve leaned down between Adam and Jack and

whispered, "You sure? We can wait."

"Shut up and sit down." Jack pushed out a chair.

Steve nudged Mark away from the vacant seat next to Jack. Didn't anyone trust Mark Richfield?

After he settled into his chair, Steve reached out over the table to Adam and said, "Hi, I'm Steve."

Adam wiped his hand on a napkin and shook Steve's hand. "Adam, Adam Lewis."

"Nice to meet you, Adam." Steve peered over at Mark. "You said Jack would be here."

"Told you." Mark giggled.

"Stop looking for me." Jack took another bite of his meal.

Adam watched their interaction very closely. It wasn't rocket science. He knew exactly what was going on. Only Mark seemed to be oblivious, or at least he pretended he was.

When the waiter showed up with their drinks, Steve and Mark ordered their food. Obviously they had been to that restaurant so often they knew what they wanted by heart.

Once they were left alone, Mark leaned over Steve just so he could annoy Jack. Adam couldn't believe Steve allowed it. The dynamics between Jack and Mark were beginning to not make as much sense as Adam originally thought. Wasn't the attraction from Jack to Mark? Not vice versa?

"Give us a taste. I love that dish," Mark goaded Jack.

"You ordered the same thing. Wait for yours." Jack continued eating, not making eye contact with anything but his food and his beer.

"Ah, Mark?" Steve nudged him to sit back. "Why don't you let Jack eat his meal? Ours will be here soon."

"Jackie-blue always used to give me a bite, right Jackie?"

"Jesus," Adam sighed, "give it a rest, Richfield."

Mark sat up, indignant. "Who the hell are you? You just joined this trio. Stop making demands."

"Trio?" both Steve and Jack echoed.

"I love all my men. I can't help it." Mark grinned wickedly, flicking back his long, thick, dark brown hair.

"Behave yourself, Mark." Steve sipped his beer. "None of us are enjoying your teasing."

"It's just good fun. I don't know why you're on me, copper. You're the one who talked about a ménage."

Adam choked on his food. Jack patted his back and offered him his water. Shaking his head, Adam indicated he was all right. "Ménage?" he repeated.

"Yes. Before Jack met you Steve asked Jack if he wanted a threesome."

Steve blushed furiously. "It was just a stupid suggestion. I didn't think anyone would take me seriously." His ale nearly gone, Steve strained over the crowd to see. "Where's the damn food?"

Adam muttered, "A suggestion to have three-way sex. Huh. What did you say, Jack?"

"I said I didn't want a sympathy fuck." Jack finished eating and set his silverware on his plate, giving his attention back to his beer.

Mark gazed at Adam intently. "What would you have said, Adam?"

"That depends."

Mark slipped Jack a suspicious look. "On what?" he pursued.

"On Jack. As far as I'm concerned, his happiness comes first. And it will always come first."

Jack gave Mark a smug look, sticking out his tongue.

"Don't do that unless you intend to use it," Mark flirted.

"Hey," Steve admonished.

"I did intend to use it," Jack shot back, "You didn't want me. But now that I have a hot lover, I'm suddenly attractive to you. Amazing how that works, isn't it, Mark?"

"It's not like that, Jackie-blue, and you know it." That pout appear again.

"Do you always use your sex appeal to manipulate

people?" Adam asked.

For some reason it made Steve roar with laughter. Mark nudged him in the ribs. "Cheeky. You are too cheeky, Adam."

"Is that another way to say I'm accurate?"

"Yes!" Steve answered loudly. "Christ, you should have seen him on our business retreat."

"Me?" Mark pressed his hands into his chest defensively. "You were the one who molested me in the desert."

"Only after you flirted with me in every meeting."

Noticing Jack growing upset, Adam interrupted them. "All right, guys."

The waiter brought Mark and Steve their appetizers, taking away Jack and Adam's empty plates. Jack ordered another beer, while Adam stuck to water.

"So? What say after dinner we all go and soak in Steve's hot tub?" Mark nibbled a chip.

"Christ, where do you come up with this shit?" Adam choked in disbelief.

"What?" Mark tried to appear innocent. "I didn't say orgy."

"Adam and I have to get up early tomorrow." Jack reclined in the chair, gazing out at the crowd on the hot deck.

"Early? On a Saturday?"

"Yes, for our workout." Jack didn't look at him.

"So? Who says you have to stay overnight?"

Steve nudged Mark. "Can't you take a hint?"

Suddenly Jack grew animated with anger. Leaning forward he snarled, "No. He can't. He's become the man who has to rub my nose in everything, haven't you, Mark?"

Adam grabbed Jack's arm, steadying him. "Jack, let's go."

"I want another beer."

"We've got a six-pack at my place." Adam threw down a handful of twenties to cover the tab.

"Don't go on my account," Mark cried. "Please. I'm sorry."

"Mark," Steve chided, "Leave them alone."

"Jackie…" Mark whined.

When Adam took a good look into Jack's face he found tears standing in his eyes. *This fucking sucks!* "Come on." Adam stood up.

Jack shoved out his chair nearly overturning the table in rage and left the patio.

Before he went, Adam glared at Mark. "Why do you have to torment him?"

"I'm not tormenting him. I love him!" Mark wiped at his eyes.

"No, you love Steve. Steve is your partner. Leave Jack alone and at least let him get over you, for Christ's sake. You have any idea how much you hurt him?"

"Yes." Mark brushed away his tears.

Steve reached for Mark, holding him tight.

"Goodbye." Adam hurried to find Jack.

Jack was leaning against the black BMW. Adam removed his keys from his pocket. Before he opened the door he caught sight of Jack's watery eyes. Cursing Mark under his breath, Adam waited until Jack climbed into the passenger seat, reaching out to hug him. When they held tight, Adam felt Jack release some of his feelings. Maybe Jack hadn't cried over Mark yet. Adam didn't know, but he did know Jack needed to now. "It's okay, baby. Let it out."

"It's not fair to you," Jack moaned.

"Forget about me. You just cry if you have to. I get it. Jack, believe me, I do." Adam tried to get over the irony of this big brawny blond needing him, holding onto him to chase away the demons. Adam was so glad to be there for him, he felt like joining Jack. But Adam would have other times to cry. This one belonged to Jack.

Adam drove them back to his home. It was Friday night

and they had no reason to get up in the morning. Why Jack had told Mark he had to get up early to work out, Adam didn't know. Other than to put him off.

Jack was silent on the drive, the tears drying on his high cheekbones. "Don't see him again," Adam wanted to say, but what good would it do? Jack wasn't seeing Mark, Mark was seeking out Jack. It was as if Mark was afraid to let go of his close companion. But what Mark didn't understand was the betrayal. Maybe he never would.

Parked at his home, Adam climbed out and waited for Jack to join him at the front door. Once they entered, Adam asked, "You want that beer?"

"No."

"Go sit outside. Stare at the ocean."

Nodding, Jack scuffed his feet to the back of the house.

While Jack was gone, Adam quickly checked his messages. Natalie had done a great job. There were only a few, and none urgent.

Meeting Jack on the back deck, Adam kicked off his loafers and dug his feet into the sand that dusted the patio. The last thing Adam wanted to do was bring up the meeting with Mark and Steve. Jack had enough. "I may have some chocolate. You want something sweet?"

Reaching out his hand, Jack clasped Adam's and replied, "I already do."

"Wow. That was nice. Thanks. But I could use a truffle."

"Go on." Jack grinned.

Racing into the house, Adam found some chocolates and brought the box outside. Sitting down on Jack's large lap, Adam fed him one before he reclined against Jack's shoulder, staring out at the cresting waves. After he chewed the candy, Adam said, "I'd never surf this time of day. They say all the great whites hunt at dusk."

"I've heard that." Jack nudged Adam for another chocolate.

Adam dropped one on Jack's tongue. "I used to surf when I was a kid. I was pretty good at it."

"I never tried it."

"Want to?"

"No. Not really."

"Anything you want to try?"

"Yes."

Adam twisted to look at him. "What?"

"Kissing you with a chocolate in your mouth."

Smiling in delight, Adam softened one on his tongue. Wrapping his arms around Jack's neck, Adam went for his lips. Inside their mouths they passed the remainder of the truffle back and forth until it dissolved. When it had, Adam kissed Jack with more passion. He was falling for him and not afraid in the least.

Jack's hands dug through Adam's thick dark hair. Adam wondered if Jack was wishing he could get lost in long locks of silky Mark-style hair. He would. Adam would let it grow. Anything for his beefy guy.

After they parted lips, Jack whispered lazily, "Thank you."

"For what?"

"For tolerating this horrible mess."

"You think you have a horrible mess?" Adam held back his laughter.

"You know what I mean."

"I do. And it's not that bad. As far as I'm concerned, this is Richfield's problem, not yours."

"You think?"

"Yes."

Jack gazed back out at the blue sea.

"Wanna fuck?"

"Yes."

"Good. Follow me to the Kasbah." Adam climbed off Jack's lap and took him and the truffles into the house. Leaving the chocolates behind, he escorted Jack to his bedroom, shutting the door behind them.

Taking off his clothing, Adam watched Jack for any signs of distress or hesitation. He couldn't see any. After he

93

had stripped, Adam found what they needed and set it on his nightstand. Jack climbed on the bed and held out his hand. "Give me a rubber."

Adam did.

Jack slid it on, reaching out his hand again.

Adam handed him the tube of lube.

Once Jack had himself prepared, Jack again beckoned, this time for Adam.

Waiting to see what Jack had in mind, Adam was maneuvered to sit on Jack's legs as Jack knelt on the mattress. Adam closed his eyes and felt Jack's shaft go deep. A shiver from a chill passed over Adam's skin. Next Jack's hand wrapped around Adam's cock. "Oh, Jack, that feels incredible"

Adam rose and fell against Jack's lap as Jack worked magic with his palm. With his eyes shut tight, Adam allowed his other senses to take over, particularly the sense of touch. Jack's breath puffed on Adam's back as his respirations increased. Under him, Jack's thighs tensed as he too set up a rhythm matching the movement of his wrist. Opening his eyes just before he came, Adam stared down at Jack's large hand surrounding his cock. Adam climaxed, choking out a grunting sound at the intensity. Jack's body shuddered inside him, jerking upwards to get in deeper.

"Oh, God…" Jack sighed.

When they had both come, Jack wrapped his arms around Adam's chest and rested his head on Adam's back. Holding Jack's massive forearms against his chest, Adam allowed the sensations to subside slowly, savoring their closeness, the unity of their bodies as they became one.

"I love you, Jack." Adam knew it was premature. Knew he shouldn't say it if they weren't ready. But he had never said it to anyone before. And the emotion seemed right at that moment with Jack's body deep inside his own. Adam knew if he didn't say it now, he never would say it to a soul.

Kisses ran along Adam's back and shoulders, his neck, his hair, as if in gratitude. Adam didn't expect to hear it back. Jack had given his love once and was burned. It would take some time, if ever, for Jack to feel comfortable uttering those three syllables again. Adam didn't mind. He didn't need to be loved to love.

Slowly they disconnected. As Adam knelt up, Jack removed the spent condom. "I'm dying of thirst. You want some water, Jack?"

"Sure."

"I'll be right back."

Jack disappeared into the bathroom.

Adam ran down to get two bottles of water, rushing back up again. Jack was sitting up in bed, under the sheets. Joining him, Adam handed him one of the cold bottles, opened his and drinking it down thirstily.

"Thanks. It hit the spot."

"No problem."

Jack wanted to say it. With all his heart he did. But he just wondered if Adam would think it was a hollow statement. Did he love Adam as much as he loved Mark? Or had loved Mark? No. So, was it fair right now to announce he did love Adam? What was enough love? Jack didn't know.

What he did know was he found a good one. A man who had a conscience, who cared, who could love, and was willing to give it without condition. That certainly did not fit Mark Richfield's description.

Chapter Six

Adam slept hard from all the physical activity. He hadn't come that many times in a night since a gay frat party in college on a dare.

The light from the sun outside began to angle in. Adam cracked open an eyelid and looked at the clock. It was after ten. Yawning, he felt Jack's warm body beside him and smiled. Was he thinking of another climax? It was like he was fifteen again.

He smoothed his hand over the rippling muscles of Jack's back. Adam admired him, imagining him as Atlas holding up the earth, or Hercules breaking marble columns. Was he Samson? And Mark his Delilah? With a man as built as Jack, the possibilities were endless.

Jack stirred under his caressing hands. Adam began kissing Jack's warm skin. Pausing, Adam tilted his head and listened carefully. Someone was ringing his doorbell.

"Jack, I'll be right back."

A low garbled noise returned from the sleepy man.

Adam stood, found a pair of jeans to slip on and a t-shirt, hopping down the stairs. Before he opened the door he looked out of the peephole first this time. "Oh, no. You have to be kidding me." Through the door, he shouted, "Go away!"

"Open this freakin' door, you traitor!"

"Get lost! I'm going to call the cops this time!"

"I spoke to my top ten! You stole them from me! They want nothin' to do with me!"

"I didn't speak to any of your top clients. I swear. If they made any decision, it was on their own."

"Open this mother-fucking door, Lewis, before I break it down!"

Adam jumped back as the screen door sounded like it broke off a hinge and then Turner's body weight began ramming the wood. "Are you insane?"

"You told my best clients I was indicted by the district court! No one knew but you, you fucking traitor!"

"No one knew but me? Oh, come on, listen to yourself!" Adam heard the door creak loudly. "Fuck!" Adam raced to the kitchen to get his cordless phone and call 911.

Jack heard noises coming from downstairs. Shouting. Banging. He sat up, grabbed his pants, and jumped into them before he raced down the stairs. "Adam?" He heard Adam's voice on the phone. Assuming he was calling the police, Jack looked out of the peephole to find Turner "You son-of-a-bitch." Turner body-slammed the door again. Before he made another attempt, Jack swung it open. Using both hands, he shoved Turner back, causing him to stumble into his Cadillac.

"Hey! Watch it!" Turner shouted, regaining his balance. "Oh, it's you."

"Yeah, it's me." Jack advanced on him menacingly. "You think you're tough, you fat piece of shit?" Standing over him, showing his teeth as he snarled, Jack poked his finger into Turner's barrel chest. "You flouting a judge's court order, Turner? Is that what you're doing? Intimidating a witness?"

"It ain't got nothin' ta do with you. It's between me and Lewis."

"Yeah?" Jack grabbed Turner's shirt collar and choked him the way Jack assumed he had choked Adam. "You don't think it's got to do with me? Think again, you maggot."

"Jack!" Adam stood in the doorway with the cordless phone. "The cops are on their way."

Jack felt Turner try to wriggle free. "Think you can run away this time, Turner?" Jack held him tighter, causing Turner to choke in a phlegm-filled cough.

"He stole my best clients. I have rights! Maybe you should look into your law books about my rights."

"You coerced innocent young men to perform sexual favors for you, and you cry about your rights? It sickens me that you do have rights, Turner. Sickens me."

"Innocent? You don't know the damn acting business, ya stupid lawyer."

Jack inched up the tension in his grip until Turner was on his tiptoes to prevent choking. "You can justify your deviance anyway you'd like, you creep. But you're still hanging around until I see handcuffs on your fat, gold-covered wrists."

"I ain't going ta jail!"

"Wanna bet?" Jack growled, baring his teeth like a wolf.

Turner shouted to Adam, "Ya got a helluvah bodyguard, don't ya, Lewis. Can't fight your own battles?"

"Hey, he's here, you came, you lose," Adam replied.

"There's only one battle, Turner," Jack sneered. "You in court being charged with violation of a court order, assault, and blackmail."

"You ain't gonna see me convicted of that. Are you nuts? That foreigner only has his fucking word against mine. There ain't no fucking witnesses."

"You know how many other clients came forward?" Jack bluffed.

Turner went pale. "No one said anyone else came forward. Who? Who else?"

"We've got a class action now. Over a dozen men have claimed you made them suck your vile cock for work."

A siren sounded in the distance.

"It was the deal. Like I said to Adam, quid pro quo. I don't do nothin' fer nothin'. They get a part. Didn't I get them parts, Adam?"

"Yup, ya sure did, Turner."

"See? It's business. I get my dick sucked and they get their roles. I can't help it if no one liked the little foreigner. Ain't because he didn't have auditions."

The patrol car skidded to a stop and two cops came rushing over. As they did, Jack released Turner. "This man is in violation of a court order. I'll show you the paperwork." He looked back at Adam. "I stuck a copy on your kitchen counter." Adam nodded and disappeared into the house.

"I didn't do nothin'. I came here to talk and this muscle-bound moron assaulted me."

One of the officers took out his handcuffs. "Put your hands behind your back, sir."

Adam raced out with the paperwork, catching his breath. One officer read it while the other one cuffed Turner.

"Let me just write down the info on my pad, okay?" the officer asked Jack.

"Take your time."

Turner went mad as the first officer tried to wedge him into the back seat of his patrol car.

"He also assaulted Mr. Lewis. He choked him." Adam approached to give the officer the details, even showing him his scratched neck.

Standing behind Adam, Jack waited until he had finished his interview and written up a quick statement.

Before the cop left, Jack asked, "Get a hook for this thing. We don't want it parked in our driveway."

"No problem." The officer smiled knowingly and got on his radio to request a tow truck.

"Hey, you remember a cop named Steve Miller?" Jack asked after the officer had finished his radio transmission.

"Sgt. Steve Miller? Yes, why?"

"He's a good friend of mine. Do you want me to tell him

you said hi?"

"Yes. Tell him to call me. It's been ages since we had a beer."

Jack read his nametag, nodding. "I will, Officer Johnson."

"Cool, thanks. A tow will be by soon to pick up the Caddy."

"Thank you." Jack waved as the officer left.

"Oh, I hope you know what you're doing." Adam said as Jack entered the house.

"I do. I got a confession out of the monster. Can't wait to call Sonja!" Jack giggled in delight and hurried to the phone.

Looking at Jack in awe, Adam smiled. "What an amazing man you are, Jack Larsen!"

Since neither of them felt motivated to do anything more than laze around after a hectic week, Adam decided they should sit on the beach and stare at the waves. Walking towards the water from the back of Adam's house, Jack carried a bag with sunscreen, a Frisbee, and bottled water. Adam had the blanket and towels.

The sun was already blazing, but the breeze coming off the water made it tolerable. Shaking out the blanket, Adam spread it along the hot sand. Kicking off his sandals, he stripped down to his bathing suit. Jack did the same, wearing only a pair of small swim trunks and his sunglasses.

Reaching into the bag, Adam removed the sun block from it before he knelt behind Jack and began coating his bronze skin. "It's nice to have one day to just veg."

"No shit. I feel like I've been going non-stop," Jack replied, letting out a deep sigh.

"Me, too. I keep losing sleep wondering what's going to happen in the future. You know, if Turner gets convicted, if he doesn't, what he'll do when he gets out of jail…"

"I know. It's hard not to think about everything."

Adam finished Jack's back, squeezing another handful of cream into his palm, spreading it on Jack's chest.

Jack sat up straighter, watching Adam's hands. "You'd think we didn't just have sex. I'm getting hard again."

Chuckling, Adam replied, "I'm in a perpetual state of arousal around you, Mr. Larsen."

"I love it." Jack took the bottle, removed his sunglasses and applied some block to his face and neck as Adam ran down Jack's arms with two hands, coating him. Next Adam did Jack's legs.

"You know this is just an excuse to touch you all over." Adam rubbed the lotion through Jack's blond leg hair.

"So? You're next, hot-stuff."

"Ooh, la la. Can't wait." He handed Jack back the bottle. "You'll use half the amount I used on you."

"You act like you're some runt. You're almost six feet tall."

"Just feel like a runt next to you, He-man."

"Oh, don't you start calling me that now as well." Jack began rubbing cream on Adam's shoulders and back.

"Sorry." Adam giggled.

"You know both Mark and Sharon call me that? Sharon even said I look like Dolf Lungren. Come on."

Adam looked over at his face. "A little."

"Get outta here."

Letting his head fall forward, Adam enjoyed the massage that accompanied the coating of the sunscreen. Jack's strong hands were kneading his sore muscles. With the rubbing and the sound of the ocean, Adam almost nodded off.

"Sit up."

Snapping awake, Adam waited as Jack smeared white stuff on his chest and stomach. "I am so fucking hard."

Jack looked around the beach. "Too many people to get naughty."

"Too bad."

While Jack finished Adam's legs, Adam took his sunglasses off, just like Jack had done, and covered his face quickly. "Did I rub it all in?"

Checking his face, Jack nodded. "You're good."

Finally doused in protective coating, they wiped their hands on a towel and lay side by side. Adam snuck his hand over to hold Jack's. Jack gripped his tight on contact.

It was bliss. The tide's constant crashing, seagulls cawing, children laughing, shouting, dogs barking, all a lull in Adam's ears he could sleep to.

The sweat running down his face and neck, Jack woke out of his slumber. The heat had put him into a coma. Sitting up, he found Adam asleep beside him. Using a towel, setting his sunglasses aside, Jack wiped the sweat off his face and then decided on a dip to cool off. Rising to his feet slowly so he wouldn't disturb Adam, the sea drew Jack with its bobbing bodies and colorful surfboards. Diving through a large wave, he surfaced on the other side and found the sand with his feet. As he rose and fell over the current, he gazed back at Adam's fantastic beach house.

His thoughts inevitably turned to Adam. The more Jack knew him, the more he adored him. And Adam's looks seemed to be blossoming as well. Adam's hair was indeed growing. The longer it got, the more adorable Adam became. No, it wasn't because of Mark. Some men just looked better with longer hair. Adam was one of them. How long would Adam allow it to grow? Jack didn't know. Shoulder length? Like Mark's?

Chiding himself for always bringing Mark to his thoughts, Jack wondered if there would come a day when either he wouldn't think of Mark, or it wouldn't matter if he did.

Getting slammed by an unexpected wave, Jack popped up and wiped the saline off his face. He didn't yearn for Mark's company. Just Adam's. That had to be a good thing.

A cold, dripping sensation woke Adam up. Shielding his eyes, Adam found a Greek god standing over him, deliberately dropping water on him. Shaking his head at that wicked grin, Adam said, "Enjoying a dip?"

Without a word, Jack bent down, grabbed Adam around the shoulders and stood him up. Once Adam was vertical, Jack tossed Adam over his shoulder, carrying him to the water.

"Hey!" Adam hollered, throwing his sunglasses back at the blanket as he was kidnapped. "You could have just asked. I would have come in." Jack's large hand smacked Adam's bottom. Adam reacted, flinching and looking around to see who was witnessing his abduction. Another slap hit Adam's rump. He hated to admit it, but he loved what Jack was doing.

Jack waded in. Adam tried to see behind him at the coming waves. Large sets of them were lurking beyond the undertow.

"Shit, Larsen!" Adam warned, seeing a monster approaching.

When it hit, Adam felt his body rise, levitating over the top of the cresting wave. After it passed he was set down on his feet to stand with Jack for the break in between.

"Feels good. I didn't realize how hot I was lying there." Adam rose over a soft wave, getting lifted off his feet. For stability, he held Jack's shoulders, using Jack as an anchor.

Jack's arm wrapped around Adam's waist, sealing them against each other under the water.

At the feel of Jack's hard-on, Adam grew very excited. Another wave crashed over them. They surfaced and shook the water out of their eyes. During the calm between, Adam cupped Jack's crotch. "You gorgeous, mother fucker."

Jack grabbed Adam's jaw and kissed him. A wave smacked Jack in the back but didn't disconnect them.

Swept away by the romance, Adam clung to Jack,

wrapping his legs around Jack's hips, his arms around Jack's neck, and seriously began sucking at his mouth and tongue. With Jack's solid weight, they rode up and down over the softer waves, knowing another mega wave would hit eventually.

When it did, it toppled them over. Adam released his hold on Jack so he could find his feet. Poking up through the surface, Adam looked around for Jack. Waiting. Suddenly hands grasped his hips. Adam was torpedoed out of the water like a rocket and thrown into the waves. Laughing wildly at the game, Adam couldn't imagine doing the same to Jack. Swimming back over to where Jack stood, Adam gripped Jack's hips and tried to lift him. Only with the help of a wave did Adam get Jack off his feet, but as far as tossing him like a ball? That wasn't going to happen. "Unfair!" Adam cracked up at how ineffective his attempts were.

"Too bad." Jack grabbed his waist and once again lifted Adam up and into a coming wave.

Even under water, Adam couldn't stop laughing. Meeting Jack, gripping him like he had previously, with his legs wrapped around Jack's waist, Adam wouldn't let him toss him away this time. "Christ, I adore you. You are so much damn fun."

Jack's blue eyes lit up with joy. As he reached out for a kiss, they were whacked again by another large wave. Holding tight, Adam waited until Jack had his footing, righting them again.

"It's rough out here!" Adam wiped the water out of his eyes.

"Yes. It is a little."

"Move us closer to shore. It doesn't look as bad there."

Walking them out step by step, Jack paused before the water dropped below their hips.

Able to stand without getting toppled over, Adam unhooked his legs from around Jack's body. Using his left hand to hold Jack close, Adam shoved his right down the

104

front of Jack's bathing suit.

"You'll get us arrested." Jack's gaze swept the shore and water.

"No one can see." Adam found his cock and balls and cupped them lovingly. "I'm really enjoying my time with you, Jack."

"Ditto, Adam."

Adam wanted to ask if they had a future, but he didn't dare. Why was the presence of Mark Richfield always looming?

"Want to lay down on the beach again, dry off? Then eat lunch?" Adam asked, massaging Jack's cock.

"Sounds good." When Adam removed his hand from Jack's swimsuit, Jack swept him into his arms and carried him to their blanket.

"You're a fucking riot, Larsen." Adam peered around them in paranoia.

"You wanted to be manhandled."

"I do, screw it." Adam hugged him, waving at a little girl who watched. "Hello!"

Jack set him down gently, finding his glasses and putting them back on his face as he relaxed beside him. "I love it here."

"Me, too." Adam put his sunglasses on as well. "You know you can stay anytime."

"Thanks, Adam."

"My pleasure, Jack."

Chapter Seven

Jack sat with Detective Blake in an office at the police station in Beverly Hills. While Jack wrote up his statement of the confession he had heard from Turner, Detective Blake waited patiently.

"Here, read it and let me know if I need to add anything." Jack handed it to him.

"You're the attorney, not me."

"But I've never had to write a statement for a crime before."

Detective Blake nodded, looking it over. "You know he's already out."

"What?" Jack asked in confusion.

"Turner. He's out on bail."

"Great. Just great. What's stopping him from bothering Adam again?"

"A court order?"

"Oh, that worked last time, didn't it?"

"Look, Jack, you know just as well as I do how this system operates."

"Can you get a conviction with that?" Jack pointed to the paper. "My statement and Logan's?"

"Not up to me. It's up to a jury."

"An LA jury, oh, goody. Crime pays in this city."

"Don't be so pessimistic. They most likely won't be keen on the look of him. And if we can get Turner on the stand to testify, they'll see what an arrogant lout he is. Have a little faith."

Nodding, Jack tried, but he didn't. He'd seen the guilty get off too many times.

After the detective looked over the statement, he said, "This is fine. I'll show it to the DA and we'll at least get something going."

"Turner won't want a trial. He'll try to settle it out of court."

"We'll see. We want jail time, and he won't settle for that. He's had one night in the county jail. Believe me, he'll fight."

"Not if he can get his cock sucked in prison."

"What?"

"Never mind. You done with me, detective?"

"I am. Thanks for your help, Jack. This has to make a difference."

"In the meantime? Hire a bodyguard for Adam?"

"He's got you," the detective replied, grinning.

"Yes, he's got me." Jack rose up, shook the man's hand. He left the precinct. Stopping on the sidewalk in front of it, he took out his cell phone. "Adam?"

"Hello, darling!"

"I just gave my statement to the police. They said Turner has already been released on bail."

"Oh, no way. Why on earth did they do that? I thought you said threats to kill were a felony."

"Don't get me started. It's just our wonderful justice system at work. How's Natalie doing?"

"She's fantastic. When I start out on my own, I'm going to offer her full-time, permanent employment."

"I'm very glad. You needed a break."

"I swear, Jack, she's got everything under control. It's like she's a natural."

"Good. Ah, Adam, now that we know Turner's out, maybe you should think about staying at my place for a few days."

107

"I can't, Jack. I've got my office here. I have to keep working."

Looking out at the busy streets, Jack felt helpless. "You want me to stay with you?"

"I can't ask you to do that. Let's not be paranoid. Maybe he got the hint. He did spend at least one night in jail. Maybe that scared him."

"Do you really want to take that chance?"

"Jack, please. Let's not get alarmed."

"You own a gun?" Jack asked.

"No."

"I'll get you one."

"Please tell me you're kidding."

"See ya later."

"Jack?"

"You just don't answer the damn door if it's him, okay? Bye, babe." Jack disconnected the phone. Checking the retail shops that lined the road, he wondered how one went about buying a firearm.

Adam hung up the phone and sighed.

"You okay, Adam?" Natalie asked.

"Yes. Sorry. Where were we?" But he was preoccupied as he listened to her query.

"I have two producers who want Isaiah Nevheg at their offices at the same time. Can you tell me which one should get priority?"

Nodding, Adam replied, "Send him to Morris. Make the other wait."

"Okay." She picked up the phone.

"If Kaplan gives you a hard time, hand him over to me."

"You got it, boss." She grinned.

Adam patted her shoulder warmly, very glad she was there. Listening to her professionalism over the phone, he knew he had gotten lucky finding her.

By five Adam waved goodbye to Natalie and packed a

few items into his workout bag. He and Jack had gotten into a routine of exercising together, eating dinner, then deciding on where to sleep, his or Jack's, for the night. It was a little hectic, but Adam was enjoying the company and the inspiration to keep up his workout regime. Locking the house, making sure the alarm was set, Adam tossed his bag into the back seat of his car and headed to Jack's place.

As he pulled up behind Jack's car in the driveway, he noticed a silver Land Rover parked out front and wondered if Mark or Steve had once again descended on the poor man. Grabbing his bag, Adam headed to the front door and knocked. Jack opened it, wearing his workout outfit, allowing him in.

The moment he entered, Adam became aware of a leggy blonde woman sitting on Jack's loveseat. "Sorry, am I interrupting something?"

"No, Adam, come in. This is Sharon Tice. Sharon, this is Adam Lewis."

Mark's Sharon? Adam gulped. *The Sharon he left standing at the altar?*

With the interest of someone looking at a snail, she glanced at Adam briefly, then as if she had been caught mid-sentence she said, "So just tell him to get lost next time, Jack. He's the biggest jerk on the planet."

"Ah," Adam cleared his throat, "I'll just go change."

Nodding, Jack gave his attention back to Sharon.

Wanting to listen to the conversation, Adam didn't go far. Standing in the bathroom, leaving the door ajar, he could hear clearly every word they said.

"I'm surprised you let him see you at all. After what he did to us?" she scoffed. "I wish I could kill the fucker. You know he had the nerve to ask for the ring back? He said it was some family heirloom. What's he going to do? Give it to Steve?"

"Did you give it back?"

"I'm still thinking about it. After all, why should I?"

"Sharon, if it's been in his family you should."

"Why do you always take his side? Jack, you never defend me. I don't get it."

Adam folded his jeans and stuffed them into the workout bag. *Because you're a whiner?*

"I'm not defending either of you. I just think you should do the right thing."

"Right thing? Are you telling *me* that? That asshole left me standing in front of all my family and friends in the middle of our wedding vows? Right thing?"

Adam cringed. Did Jack need all this rehashing going on? Wasn't it bad enough that Mark and Steve were doing it?

"Sharon, you don't think I know what happened? I was there, remember? I was also there when the two of us suspected he and Steve were screwing. Why do we have to keep going on and on?"

Exactly! Adam was ready, dressed in his shorts and t-shirt, but couldn't resist eavesdropping on the conversation.

"Because you keep seeing him," Sharon argued. "Why? Why do you let him come by? You're a lawyer, get an order to keep him away."

"Sharon."

Adam perked up to the seriousness of Jack's voice.

"Are you just upset that he's coming here, and not going to your place trying to be friends with you?"

Ahh, Adam nodded. *Makes sense*. A long silence followed. Adam wondered if Jack was waiting to be rescued.

Then Sharon said, "I'm leaving."

"Don't be mad at me over it," Jack replied.

"I hate all of you. I don't know why I came."

Neither do I. Adam shook his head. The sound of the door shutting soon followed. Adam poked his head around the corner. Jack was standing next to it, his hand still holding the door knob as if it were propping him up.

Feeling sorry for Jack for having to be reminded of events he'd sooner forget, Adam dropped his workout bag down and approached him. "You okay, babe?"

"Hmm?"

"Jack?" Adam wondered where Jack's thoughts were. If he had to guess, he'd say standing in that wedding hall, wearing a tuxedo while Sharon was jilted at the altar.

"Right. Let's get started." Jack walked to the gym.

Shutting his mouth, knowing he'd come by last Friday and didn't want to talk about his ordeal either, Adam followed him. When Jack was ready, he'd initiate the conversation on his own.

Jack wanted to move away. Maybe leave the country. He couldn't seem to shake off the reasons that made him feel so depressed. And it seemed everyone who had been a part of that horrible wedding-that-never-was kept rehashing the event, even though it had occurred months ago. Yes, it was a nightmare, but did it have to be a re-occurring one?

Stretching in front of the mirrors to warm up, Jack noticed Adam as he set up the treadmill. He wondered how much of the conversation Adam had heard. It didn't matter. Adam knew all the sordid details of that day.

Smiling to himself, Jack crossed the room, around the plethora of equipment, and stood next to Adam as the belt began to move and his workout began.

Adam held onto the side rails, his feet picking up speed, and asked, "Yes?"

Reaching across the bar to him, Jack grabbed Adam's face and kissed his lips. Adam struggled to jog, hold on, and kiss Jack simultaneously. When Jack parted from the kiss, Adam shouted, "You trying to kill me, Larsen?"

"No, on the contrary." Jack winked at him, getting back to his warm up. Seeing Adam in the mirror's reflection, he caught his adoring smile and sighed happily.

While they were out to dinner at a restaurant, Jack's

mobile phone rang. Thinking he had shut it off, he gave Adam a pained look.

Adam shrugged. "Don't ignore it on my account."

Taking it out of his pocket, Jack read the display and said, "Oh, it's Sonja." He hit the button to answer it. "Hello, lady. What's up?"

"Sorry to bother you, Jack. I just wanted to tell you the DA has offered Turner a deal."

"Oh?" Jack made eye contact with Adam.

"They offered him five years jail time, ten years probation, and prohibited him from contacting clients alone if he continues to act as an agent."

"He'll never go for it."

"I don't know. With the felony violation, threats to kill, added to his charges, he could look at twenty years."

"I'm telling you, he'll refuse."

"What?" Adam asked and stopped chewing his pasta.

"Probably. Well, we'll all be in court then," Sonja said.

"When's the DA offering him the deal?"

"He did earlier today."

"My guess is it'll be set for trial next month."

"All right, Jack. I just wanted to let you know what's going on."

"Okay, Sonja. Thanks." He disconnected the call and relayed to Adam, "They offered Turner five years in jail."

Adam laughed sadly. "He'll never take it."

"No. I didn't think so either."

"Oh, well. You know, Jack, I'm really not happy about everyone finding out I've been privy to all this crap and did nothing. You realize I'll go bankrupt."

"We'll ask for a closed courtroom. Besides, you didn't do anything. He did."

"Will it matter if the courtroom is closed? Gossip in this town spreads like fire in hay. No way, Jack."

"If it does get out, and you can't get back into the same work, you know, as an agent. What would you want to do?"

"Do? I don't want to do anything else. I really love this

job. I get off on the racing around, getting actors roles, contracts, movies. No, there's nothing else I would like to do."

"Don't want to be Mrs. Larsen?"

Blinking in shock, Adam swallowed his food first before he laughed. "Can't I be a working wife?"

"Sure, baby. You can be anything you want." Jack reached out for his hand.

"Wow, Mr. Larsen. You sure know how to drop bombs on me."

"Keeps you on your toes."

"Kissing you keeps me on my toes."

"Will you stop! You're not short!" Jack peered around the crowded restaurant. "You really need to stop referring to yourself as little. You're larger than average."

"Maybe shoe lifts."

Nudging him, Jack shook his head at his antics. "Okay, tiny, get shoe lifts."

"Tiny?" Adam stuck out his chest.

"You're the one who thinks he's small, not me."

"I'm not small!"

"No, you're not. Especially where it counts."

"Eat faster. I'm already hard."

Jack took a large mouthful of food, grinning at him.

Adam unlocked his door, trying to dodge Jack's hands. Charging up the staircase with Jack in pursuit, Adam was laughing so hard he was gasping for breath. They had teased each other all through dinner, the drive home, and now inside Adam's house.

Tossing his leather jacket on the floor, Adam used the bed as a shield between him and the raging bull. "Stay back, He-man."

"Make me." Jack made a quick maneuver to go around the bed, faking Adam out. Adam started running, then backed up and waited for Jack's next move.

"I'll lock myself in the bathroom."

"Not if I can get to you first." Jack rushed him.

Adam jumped on top of the mattress and off the other side.

"Cheater!" Jack shouted.

"What? Are you kidding me? Anything goes with you, Samson!"

Moving slowly, Jack took a step towards him. Adam shifted in the opposite direction. Jack pounced on the bed, over it, and swooped down on Adam.

Adam was choking with laughter. Jack lifted him over his head, dropping Adam down on the springy mattress. Once Adam had stopped bouncing, Jack pinned him down with his body weight, opening Adam's jeans.

Through his hysteria, Adam could not prevent Jack from stripping his lower half. The amount of pressure Jack used to push Adam into the bed was astounding, and it was just Jack's chest. No matter how Adam squirmed, reached, grappled, he was being undressed. "Augh! No fair! I need help!"

"Ha! Gotcha where I want ya." Jack yanked Adam's briefs down with his jeans to his knees, exposing him.

When Jack cupped his genitals lightly, Adam settled down to a more passive resistance. Jack's face hovered over his. Reaching for his blond waves, Adam drew Jack to his lips. As he swirled his tongue around Jack's mouth, Jack's hand dug between Adam's thighs, under his balls. The chills it sent over Adam made his cock go rock hard.

"Fuck me, Samson." Adam caught his breath.

Sitting back, letting up on the pressure on Adam's ribs, Jack finished undressing Adam.

Adam lay naked on the bed, recuperating from their roughhousing.

Standing next to the bed, Jack unbuttoned his shirt, his stare never leaving Adam's exposed body.

Once he was naked as well, Jack crept between Adam's thighs and nuzzled in between his legs. Instinctively Adam

114

spread wide, inviting more. Closing his eyes, Adam felt the gooseflesh rise on his arms as Jack's coarse jaw rubbed against the soft skin of his inner thighs. Jack's hot mouth sucked one of Adam's testicles. Adam groaned out loud. "Oh, Larsen, you are something else."

More wet heat surrounded his balls, first one, then the other, each getting a tongue swirling and tickling against them. Adam writhed.

That masterful tongue made its way to Adam's cock. The licking up and down continued until he was enveloped by Jack's hot mouth. Adam's body rocked in reflex, becoming a fucking machine against his will. He couldn't have stayed still if someone had super-glued him to the bed.

Pushing deeply into Jack's mouth, Adam came.

Swallowing down his come in pleasure, Jack used the back of his hand to wipe his mouth. While he knelt between Adam's legs Jack gazed at the expression of nirvana on Adam's face. Adam's dark hair stuck to his sweat coated forehead, Jack thought he couldn't look any more beautiful.

Jack reached to the nightstand for a condom. He slipped it on and gently elevating Adam's legs to his shoulders. Propping Adam's hips up on a pillow, Jack slid in, closing his eyes, hissing a breath of air through his teeth. Screwing him slowly with gentle thrusts, Jack felt his skin ignite. In moments he was exploding with a sensation of pure pleasure.

Hanging his head, catching his breath, Jack opened his eyes. Adam's deep brown irises seemed to glow in the dim room. Jack didn't know why, but if felt right to say, "I love you, Adam."

A look of surprise appeared on Adam's face.

Connected to Adam, not wanting to pull out, Jack paused to savor it. With care Jack lowered Adam's legs down to the bed, one at a time, finally backing up to break their contact. Taking off the used condom, Jack was about

115

to get up to toss it in the bathroom trash, when Adam sat up and hugged him.

Letting it drop to the floor, Jack returned the embrace, holding on tight, sniffing Adam's cologne, kissing his hair.

"Oh, Jack…"

"I know, Adam, I know."

Chapter Eight

Adam rushed around with Cassidy, his client, chauffeuring him to a few meetings to give him some confidence. He was relatively new and had been through what most of Turner's clients had experienced, and was now petrified everyone in Tinsel Town would know he sucked cock for his auditions. It wasn't the first nervous young man Adam had escorted to his appointments, and until this whole torrid event passed, it wouldn't be the last.

"You'll be fine. Believe me, Cassidy, everyone knows Turner. No one will think badly of you. Just get in there and look confident."

"Are you coming in?"

"Yes. I'll be right with you." Adam patted his back as they neared the entrance of the building. His mobile phone rang. "Adam Lewis, how can I help you?"

"You can get that freakin' lawyer of yours to recount his statement."

Adam looked at the display on his mobile phone. It didn't read Turner's number, reading unlisted instead. "What the hell do you want from me?"

"Five years? You think I'm doin' five years in the slammer? You gotta be kiddin'."

Adam suddenly felt paranoid he might get hit with a sniper bullet. Rushing Cassidy into the lobby of the building, Adam gestured for him to push the elevator button. "Where are you, Turner?"

"None of your business. Now, what's it gonna take to get that brawny asshole off my back? How much?"

"Forget it. He won't take a bribe. Do yourself a favor. Check in for some psychiatric help, and maybe they'll reduce the sentence. I have to go." Adam disconnected the call as they stepped into the elevator.

"Was that him?"

"Yes. Forget about it. He's my problem, not yours."

"He's become everyone's problem, Adam."

Trying to give Cassidy a reassuring smile, Adam held his shoulder as they made their way down the hall.

"Jack."

Jack paused as he walked down the hall of the courthouse. It was District Attorney Aiden. He approached her, both of them moving to the side of the corridor to speak privately.

"Turner is claiming you used force to coerce his confession."

"Of course he is."

"Did you? Did you do anything to him to make him talk?"

"No. Don't be absurd. You don't know this guy. He's damn proud of his business practices. He doesn't think there's anything wrong with it."

"It's not the first time I've heard of it either, Jack. It's just that it rarely comes into the spotlight like this. No one is coming forward. You think all those straight men in the acting profession want to admit what they did?"

"No. Of course they don't. I know that. This Logan Naveah has balls, believe me."

"The poor thing. I can't believe no one will come out and back him on it. Without your testimony, you realize the kid's got nothing but his word."

"I know."

"You sure you want to get involved at that level?"

"Yes. Very sure."

"What about Adam Lewis?"

Jack bit his lip in frustration. "I didn't think he had any good info for the prosecution. Wasn't he discounted as a witness?"

"Not for us, for the defense."

"What?" Jack looked around the hall quickly. "The defense? What the hell's that all about?"

"I think Arthur Harris is going to use some kind of switch and bait tactics."

"They're going to try and blame Adam?"

"Complicity. Make Adam Lewis out as the same ilk as Turner."

"Shit." Jack felt ill. "I don't want him to go through that."

"I didn't think so. Should we cut a different deal?"

"No. Let me talk to Adam first. Don't do anything yet."

"I really think even though Mr. Lewis has never assaulted anyone, the media, the critics, as well as the jury, may perceive him as guilty by association."

"Can't the prosecutor set up some shield prior to Adam's cross? You know, like somehow advising the jury that this is a tactic that will be used to deflect guilt off Turner?"

"You know he can try. How successful it'll be is up to the jury."

"Well, I'm defending Adam myself, so if Prosecutor Mia can't do it, I will."

"Okay, Jack. I have to go."

"Thanks, Isabella. I appreciate it."

He waved as he walked away. Jack didn't want Adam to go through any more agony. No way.

By five Jack entered his home, still thinking about Adam coming for their workout and trying to convince him that maybe Logan and he should reconsider this accusation before everyone but Turner got nailed.

Changing out of his suit, Jack checked his answering machine. No one had left a message. It had been three days since Mark tried to contact him. It was a miracle.

Dressed in his shorts and tank top, Jack went through what was becoming a ritual of getting bottled water and towels, and picking out a CD.

When the doorbell rang, Jack had a thought. Heading to the kitchen cabinet first, he located the old key Steve had relinquished to him, and brought it to hand to Adam. Palming the key, Jack opened the door.

"Hiya, babe." Adam smiled as he stepped inside.

"Hello, sweetie. Here. Take this. No need to keep ringing the bell."

"A key?"

"Yes. Just keep it."

Taking it, staring at it as if it was a magic wand, Adam was speechless.

Jack smiled at him adoringly and made his way to the gym. "I'll be waiting!"

"Okay!"

Adam dropped his gym bag in the bathroom and twisted Jack's house key around his own key ring. It was a huge step. Stuffing it into his pocket, Adam changed his clothing, then went to meet Jack in the workout room.

"U2 or Jethro Tull?" Jack held, two CDs in his hand.

"Ah, which Tull?"

"Thick as a Brick."

"Tull." Adam stretched his back muscles a little, stepping on the treadmill as Jack started the CD. Though he wanted to exchange the usual, "How was your day, honey?", it had to wait. Adam knew for Jack the workout was paramount. Talking could go on anytime. And ironically, working out with Jack every day, Adam soon had the same credo. Not to mention the news that Turner had contacted him again would anger Jack so much, it didn't need to happen before the workout routine. Jack should be allowed his time to de-stress.

Moving the speed up quickly, Adam was soon jogging at nice easy pace, growing stronger and running longer and faster each time. As Jack heft unimaginable weights over his head, Adam smiled in pleasure, remembering those three tiny little words Jack had uttered. It made so much of a difference to Adam that he felt he had changed as a person. No one said that sentence to him. Not since he was a little boy in Vancouver and his mom did. This man loved him. How cool was that?

An hour later, Adam was drenched in sweat, having run six miles and done close to a hundred sit-ups. Drained, he lay back on the mat and recuperated while Jack finished up putting back the plates of weight he had been using. Once the room was made neat and the music system closed down, Jack stood over Adam smiling at him.

"Hello, Samson."

"At least you're not calling me He-man."

"No. That name's been overused." Adam reached toward him for help in standing. Jack hauled him up so quickly, Adam almost flew into the air. "You think I should lift weights?"

Picking Adam up in his arms, Jack cradled him close. Adam instinctively wrapped his legs around Jack's hips and his hands around his neck. "No."

"Why not? Afraid of some healthy competition?" Adam rubbed his nose against Jack's.

"No. I love you the way you are."

Adam belted out the Billy Joel lyrics, shutting up when Jack raised a skeptical eyebrow at him. "No good?"

"Don't quit your day job."

"I never claimed to be a good singer."

"You're not horrible, but you're no Greg Lake."

"Your hard-on is poking me." Adam wriggled.

"Can't help it. You turn me on."

121

"Still, you turn me on…" Adam sang.

"Nope, you're still no Greg Lake."

"Oh, well. You going to hold me like this all night?"

"Maybe." Jack got a tighter grip on Adam's body.

"Screw me standing up?"

"Maybe."

Adam rested his head on Jack's shoulder. When he did, Jack rocked him side to side gently. Seeing them like that in the mirror suddenly, Adam had to laugh. "What a pair we make."

Jack twisted around so he could see their reflection. "What? We make a great pair."

"You think?"

"Yes." Jack allowed Adam to slip down to get to his feet. Standing side by side, Adam inspected their features, seeing if their looks complimented each other. "I suppose."

"Shut up. Let's shower and eat. I'm starved."

Adam grabbed his water bottle as he left, finishing the remainder. "What's on the menu?"

"Didn't I choose last time?"

"Nope. I did."

"You sure?"

"Yes." Adam smacked Jack's bottom as he stood near the shower stall starting the water.

"Okay. Redondo Beach pier. There's a great seafood place there."

"Cool."

"Now get in the shower so I can screw you." Jack nudged him.

"Yes sir!" Adam saluted him comically.

Jack drove them to the waterfront, parking the car in a pay lot. He had a lot on his mind but wanted to wait until they had opened a bottle of wine before he started that dreaded conversation.

Adam waited for Jack to catch up as Jack fed the parking

box, arming the car with a chirp of his key fob. Walking together to the restaurant Jack came to a halt. Adam had stopped short appearing to read something that was posted to a tree near the lot. "What are you doing?"

"Look. It's a picture of Angel Loveday. You remember that guy?"

Jack stood behind Adam's shoulder to see it. "Christ! That's obscene. I'm surprised they allowed that to be posted in a public place."

Adam touched the paper. "It's just some flimsy print-out. It doesn't feel like poster paper."

"Poor guy. I wonder if he even knows it's there." Jack tugged it down.

"I loved his movies. You remember any of them?" Adam asked, resuming their walk.

Jack tossed the paper into a trashcan and then thanked some patrons who were leaving as they held the restaurant door for them. "Oh, yes. I remember them. Loved *Lust*. I think I still own it on VHS somewhere."

"You kidding me? You actually have one of his old movies? Well, we need to watch it! Great foreplay."

"Deal." Jack smiled at him, waiting in line for the hostess to acknowledge them.

Once they were seated and had menus in their hands, Jack tried to come up with some way of broaching the topic that he was loath to discuss. Turner. What a better way to ruin one's appetite. But there was no good time to talk about him. If he waited until later then it would ruin the rest of their evening. So it was now or never.

Adam could tell Jack was preoccupied. When Jack had things on his mind, he had the habit of looking around the room and not directly at Adam. Once they had ordered a bottle of blush wine, Adam sipped his water. "Out with it."

"Huh?"

"Don't look so surprised. I know something's on your

123

mind. What did Mark do now?"

"No. It's not about Mark."

Moving his legs so he touched Jack's under the table, Adam leaned back in his chair. "Steve?"

"No. Adam, I have something important to discuss with you."

"You're breaking it off with me?" Adam's heart ached.

"No! Shut up and listen."

Adam said, "Phew!" in exaggeration, wiping his brow.

"I had a chat with the DA today. We ran into each other in the courthouse."

"Oh." Adam had his own Turner update, but knew it could wait.

"She warned me that you would be put through some crap on the witness stand."

"I thought I didn't have enough to help the prosecution?"

The waiter appeared with their wine. Jack nodded to the bottle. The waiter opened it, pouring a sample. Nodding again, Jack waited until he filled both glasses and left.

"Jack," Adam urged, "what's going on?"

"You're going to be called as a witness for the defense."

"The defense? What makes them think I will defend Turner?"

"They want to make it out that you were as guilty as he is."

Adam blinked. About to sip his wine, he set it back on the table. "How can they do that?"

"Juries are gullible, Adam. You know that. My guess is if Arthur Harris has his way, he'll put enough doubt in their minds that they may feel Turner isn't guilty unless you are, and let him off."

"I didn't molest anyone!"

Jack looked around the room. He whispered softly, "Calm down."

Adam took a long drink of the wine, fuming.

"I want you and Logan to think very carefully about this.

It may come back to bite you both."

"First of all, Jack, I didn't initiate this charge. Logan did. Okay? Secondly, I didn't do anything. I never assaulted anyone."

"But you didn't stop it. You didn't go to the police."

"Jack!"

"Adam, these aren't my words. They are going to be Turner's lawyer's words."

"You'll be there to defend me. To object to that line of questioning." Adam felt the sweat break out on his forehead and raised the bottle to pour himself another glass of wine.

"I can object all I want. The judge will allow some of it, I guarantee. Even if he gives Harris a short leash, the jury will inevitably hear you knew. You knew and did nothing."

"What was I to do? Huh?" Adam felt his veins protruding. "Okay, great. If I went to the cops and no victim came forward, then what? What the hell was I supposed to do? I knew these guys didn't want that act acknowledged. You think I was going to put pressure on them? They had enough crap to deal with. This business is brutal as it is."

"They may want to know why you stuck by Turner for ten years."

That was the straw that broke Adam's back. He rose up, grabbing his jacket off his chair. Immediately Jack grabbed his arm, stopping him. "Sit down."

"It's you who's asking it, not some jerk named Harris. Right, Jack? You want to know why I stuck it out? You!"

Very calmly, Jack repeated, "Sit down."

Adam threw his coat back over the chair and dropped down.

The waiter appeared. "Is everything all right?"

"Yes," Jack smiled, "fine."

"Are you ready to order?"

"No, could you give us another few minutes?"

Meanwhile, Adam brooded, arms crossed, getting ready to scream.

Once they were alone again, Jack reached over and

dragged those tightly wound arms down and held Adam's hands across the table. "It is not me who is asking. I know you love what you do. I also know you did your best to stay out of it and would have been there for those men if they had asked you for help."

The grip on his hands and the sensible words began to soothe Adam. He released his tight back muscles.

Jack continued, "This is why I am talking to you now, Adam. I want you to think about what might happen in a courtroom. Turner may walk out unscathed and you and Logan could be branded for life."

"How unfair is that?"

"Very. But it's not impossible."

"What the hell should I do, Jack? If I back out and Turner gets all the charges dropped, then Logan and I look like idiots, Turner gets his business back, and I'm out of a damn job scrounging around for leftover clients. And he has so much power out there, I won't get a scrap. I have to go through with this. I have no fucking choice."

"Fine. I just want you to know what you're up against. Yes, I will be there. Yes, I will defend you, object to dirty tactics, you know that. I will fucking battle dragons for you, Adam. But even I cannot prevent what might happen if Harris goes in that direction."

Jack's grip on his hands released. Adam raised his wine glass to his lips again, sucking the alcohol down.

"You okay?"

"No. But I understand." He gave the room a quick glance. No one was interested in them. "Turner called again. He called my cell phone while I was with a client on our way to a meeting." Predictably Jack's face hardened. "He told me to get you to drop your statement. I just told him to fuck off and get mental help."

"We need to write it up as another violation."

"Forget it. What's the use?"

"The use is, the more we have going in, the more ammo we have coming out."

126

The waiter appeared again. "Are you ready to order yet?"

Jack handed him the unread menus. "Two lobster tails with the filet mignon, and a side salad."

"Thank you, sir."

Adam grinned. "Wow. That's a celebration meal. You sure you want to have that now and not after we lose the trial?"

"We won't lose." Jack raised his wine glass. "To us. Fuck everyone else."

Adam tapped Jack's glass. "I love you to death, Jack Larsen."

"And I love you to life, Adam Lewis."

Chapter Nine

"He hasn't called in a bloody week," Mark complained.

"Will you leave him alone?" Steve stood behind Mark. "You're behaving like a damn stalker. Just plug this info into the damn computer and stop whining."

"I do not whine. Why does everyone think I whine! It's a horrible thing to say." Mark began typing on the keyboard.

"He's just met someone. When a relationship is new, the people in it need time to bond. Jack and Adam don't need us hanging around."

"But I miss him."

"I know, baby." Steve touched Mark's long hair. They were in Mark's office and the door wasn't closed.

"You think he'll ever forgive me?"

"Sure. Just wait awhile. More than a damn week."

"You're all so mean."

"Us? Oh, Richfield, you sometimes act delusional." Steve snuck a kiss to Mark's head before they continued working. "Keep typing."

"He calls me delusional, then tells me to keep working."

"You'll get it tonight if you misbehave," Steve warned.

"Oh?" Mark shot him a wicked glance.

"Stop or we won't get anything done."

"Will you wear your police uniform for me again?"

Chuckling softly, Steve replied, "Anything you want."

"Yum!" But Mark's gaze moved to the phone on his

desk. The urge to call Jack was overpowering.

Adam sat on his back patio with his mobile phone to his ear. Natalie was busy working upstairs in the study. "Logan, I'm just telling you what my lawyer said."

"But why does my lawyer say something else. Can't we all have the same lawyer?"

"No. We all have to have our own representation. What does your lawyer say?"

"He told me that now that we have a confession, there's nothing to worry about."

"Oh?" Adam tried to feel hopeful, but he knew Jack's opinion had more clout.

"So, now all of a sudden, you want me to drop the charges?"

"No. No, Logan, I don't. I'm not telling you what to do. I'm just telling you what my attorney said."

"What do you think we should do?"

"Go for it. I think we've come this far we can't back out."

"Right. That's it then. We go."

"Okay, Logan. As long as you know what's at stake."

"I do. I did when I first made the decision to speak out about it."

"You're a very brave man, Logan."

"No. I'm just sick of that practice. Someone has to do something."

"Go get 'em, tiger." Adam laughed.

"Thanks for all your support, Adam. I don't know what I'd do without you."

"No problem. We just have to stick together. See ya." Adam hung up, staring out at the tide and the clouds looming over the ocean. At the moment they were blocking out the hot sun. Just as he was standing up to check on Natalie, his cell phone rang. "Hello?"

"Mr. Lewis?"

"Yes?" Adam heard the thick accent and knew it sounded familiar.

"I know about the trial involving Jack Turner."

Adam sat back down, his heart rate rising. "And?"

"I want to come forward as well. He did it to me and it made me sick."

"Who is this?"

"I don't want to say at the moment."

"Ewan! Ewan Gallagher!"

"Oi? Me northern tongue gave me away. 'ullo, Adam."

"Oh, Ewan, I can't tell you how relieved I am that you're doing this."

"It's the least I can bloody do. What a fucking wanker Turner is. I can't let it go. But please, Adam, don't tell anyone who it is. Would you keep it to yourself, mate?"

"Yes. I understand, Ewan, believe me. Can I have you call my lawyer? There may be a way to do this without your identity being revealed."

"There is, love. I've already obtained a lawyer. I just wanted you to know."

"This is great news, Ewan. Thank you. You sure you want to do this? Have you discussed it with Jason? You both know the risks?"

"Yes. We've discussed it, Adam. We know. I'm not in Hollywood any longer, and he sure as shite can't do anything about me way out here in Carlisle. Yes. I'm sure. I want to get that bastard."

Adam felt so relieved, he stood up and pumped his hand into the air in victory. "Great. Thank you, Ewan! Oh, can I at least have the name of your lawyer? To tell my lawyer?"

"Bernstein. Jennifer Bernstein."

"Yes. Great. Thanks again, Ewan." He hung up and shouted, "Yahoo! Way to go Jennifer!"

"Oh, Mr. Larsen?"

"Yes, Mrs. Bernstein?" Jack stopped his progress down

the hall. Responding to her craning finger, Jack followed her to her office.

"Have a seat."

"What did I do now?"

"Nothing. Why? What are you guilty of?" She grinned slyly.

"Never mind. What's up?"

"Another victim of Mr. Turner's has shown up."

"No!"

"Yes. I'm representing him."

"Who is it?"

"He requests anonymity. But he's a good one. Have no doubt. You remember the actor Ewan Gallagher?"

Jack felt his skin prickle at the name, recalling what Adam had said about making a move on Ewan's lover, Doctor Jason Phillips. It gave him some perspective on how Adam was feeling about Mark. Jealousy. "Yes. How did you get them to come forward?"

"I made a call to England, just on the off chance he would offer. He's not in the States anymore, and it certainly wouldn't affect his career."

"Oh, Jen, this is such good news!" Jack took out his cell phone, indicating to Jennifer to wait as he dialed. "Hello? Adam?"

"Jack, you'll never guess what just happened."

"Wait, let me tell me my news first!"

"No! Come on!"

"Adam," Jack shouted, "another witness came forward!"

"Yes! Jennifer is defending him!"

"I know! How do you know?" Jack started laughing, winking at Jennifer where she sat on the corner of the desk, a smug smile on her lips.

"I just got a call from the guy. We got him now, Jack, right?"

"We're closer, Adam." Jack heard him whooping it up. "I'll find out more and get back to you."

"Can't wait. See you at your place for our workout."

"Yup!" Jack disconnected the line and grinned at Jennifer. "Let's find Sonja and head to the DA's office."

Jennifer grabbed her purse. "Let's go!"

Rushing up the stairs to Natalie, finding her on the phone, Adam waited patiently as she made an appointment, typing onto the calendar simultaneously. When she hung up, she asked, "You okay?"

"I'm great." He pulled over a chair and sat next to her. "Look, you're fantastic. You've picked this up so well, can I offer you permanent employment? And a raise?"

"Are you kidding?" she gasped.

"No. You like the work?"

"I love it!"

"I'm so glad to hear it. Natalie, I don't know what I would have done without you this past week."

She reached out to him for a hug. He wrapped around her plump form and squeezed tight. After they broke the embrace, he said, "Eventually we'll have a proper office. Not just working from here."

"Okay."

"I'll make sure we get you health insurance and some extra benefits. I'll take good care of you."

"Thanks, Adam. I really like the job. I can't believe all the stars I get to work with."

He smiled. "It is fun, isn't it?"

"Yes! Thanks again."

"No, thank you. You've really made my life easier."

A small crowd gathered in the DA's office. Jack listened carefully as Jennifer told them about the new witness. Once she had, the DA told the prosecutor, "Aubrey, find out if Arthur Harris is in the courthouse. Let's get him in here and advise him on this new development. Then offer a ten year prison deal, ten years probation, no resuming of his agency, and no bargaining."

Jack, Jennifer, and Sonja exchanged grins.

The prosecutor nodded and left the room.

"Have we got him, Isabella?" Jennifer asked.

District Attorney Aiden smiled, "We've got him, Mrs. Bernstein."

Arthur Harris did not like what he was hearing. Nodding his head, he told the prosecutor, "Let me call my client." After Prosecutor Mia left, Harris dialed his cell phone. "Turner?"

"Yeah?"

"Bad news."

"What now?"

"Someone else came forward as a witness for the prosecution."

"Who? I'll kill him!"

"They said they would remain anonymous."

"And? What now?"

"Now they want ten years if we settle out of court."

"Ten? What the fuck happened to five?"

"They have a stronger case, Turner. Two witnesses, your confession, and whatever Lewis can give them." Silence followed. "Take it, Turner. Or you'll end up with twenty."

"Take it? You gotta be kiddin'? I ain't goin' to the joint!"

"Look, it's my job to advise you. And I think this is the best deal you'll get."

"Tell 'em I'll go to rehab! Tell 'em two years and some counseling."

"Two years?"

"Look, get us all in a room. Get me a meeting. I need to bargain. You ain't worth shit."

"Fine."

Adam couldn't wait to see Jack. Using his key, Adam opened Jack's front door, shouting, "Hello?" Listening for a reply, Adam entered the house, shouting, "Jack?" Setting his bag down outside the door of the gym, Adam hopped up the staircase, looking for his lover. "Oh, Jack?"

"Adam?"

"Yes." Adam found Jack in his room, holding a handgun. "Holy crap!"

"Here. I got this for you."

"I don't want it!" Adam held up his hands.

"Just keep it in your house. As the noose begins to tighten around Turner's neck, he's going to start getting more insane."

"But a gun? A gun, Jack? Is that really necessary?" Adam was afraid to touch it.

"Please. It would give me some peace of mind."

"Is it loaded?"

"No." Jack opened the chamber of the revolver, showing the empty barrel.

Adam took it from him, the gun appearing slightly less deadly with its empty guts hanging out. Feeling the unexpectedly heavy weight in his hand, Adam shook his head. "I've never even held one before."

"It's not that complicated, Adam. Point and shoot."

"Yeah, sure." Adam studied the small, two-inch barrel of the thirty-eight caliber Smith and Wesson. "I need to learn how to use it."

"Steve can teach you."

"Oh, yes. Right. He can, can't he? Do you think he would?" Adam asked curiously.

"Yes." Jack pointed to a box of bullets. "Take those with you. When you get home, load it."

"Are you sure this is necessary?" Adam set the gun down on the bed next to the bullets.

"You won't stay here, I work during the day, and you're alone all day while you're working with Natalie. So, yes, it's necessary."

"What's Steve's number?" Adam didn't even want to touch the thing without instruction.

Jack walked over to his nightstand and picked up the phone. "Hello? Mark? Let me talk to Steve. Because I want to talk to Steve, not you!"

Adam cringed. "Jack, forget it."

Jack shot Adam an annoyed expression then said into the phone, "Steve? I have a special favor to ask you."

Sitting down on the bed next to the gun, Adam felt his stomach flip. Was Turner that violent? Weren't his threats all talk, like everything about him? Adam had known Turner for a decade, surely he wouldn't be capable of killing him. Or vice versa.

"Could you? I'd appreciate it. No, alone. Why the hell does Mark have to follow you everywhere? I know, Steve, but just this once?"

Rubbing his face, Adam wished every aspect of his life wasn't complicated.

When Jack hung up, he relayed to Adam, "He's coming over after our workout, in about an hour and a half."

"Okay." Adam stood, intending on getting changed into his gym clothing.

A hand held him back. Turning to look at Jack, Adam caught the expression of worry in his eyes. Embracing Jack warmly, Adam sighed, resting his head against his shoulder. "I hope this blows over soon. I feel as if it's escalating and I don't know if it's just our imaginations."

"I want you safe, Adam."

"Okay, Jack. I understand."

"Let me come with you!"

"No!" Steve grabbed his keys.

"Steve! It's not fair. Why do you get to see them? What harm would it do if I just hung out in the background?"

"You never hang out in the background, Mark. You have to be the center of attention."

"I'm going."

"Jack asked for me to come alone."

"I don't care. I'll follow you there in my car."

"You're being ridiculous."

"And you're being a putz! Now let's go." Mark opened the front door.

"Richfield, you really are a stubborn mother fucker." Steve sighed.

"How long have you known me? You're just figuring that out now?"

"Shut up. If Jack gets angry, you deal with it. Not me."

"I will. Don't worry."

Adam dressed in his casual clothing, feeling refreshed after the workout and shower. Jack was in the bedroom, finishing up, tucking his shirt into his pants. When the doorbell sounded, they both perked up. "Steve's here," Jack announced.

Adam descended the stairs behind Jack. "I bet Mark's with him."

Hearing a deep exhale from Jack, Adam assumed Jack figured he would be as well.

Waiting as Jack answered the door, Adam first made eye contact with the handsome ex-cop, then heard Jack say, "Why are you here?"

"I knew it," Adam mumbled.

"Jackie! I won't get in the way. What is it you want from Steve anyway? I thought you hated him as much as you hated me."

"Go home, Mark. You're already irritating me."

Steve gave Mark an I-told-you-so glance, then asked Jack, "What can I do for you?"

"I want you to show Adam how to use a firearm."

"Okay."

Adam met Steve's steel-blue eyes, read the confidence in them instantly, and did feel relieved.

"Where's the gun?" Steve asked.

"Up in my bedroom. Adam, can you show him where it is?"

Nodding, Adam started heading towards the staircase. Jack's body language changed to fury as he confronted the bane of his life.

As they climbed to the second floor, Adam muttered, "He just couldn't be left behind."

"Nope. You know Mark. I tried, honest."

"I'm sure you did. I just feel bad for Jack."

"Jack can handle Mark, believe me."

Adam agreed with that statement, to a point, but didn't want to discuss anything further with Steve. "There. There it is on the dresser."

Steve immediately picked it up and opened the barrel to check if it was loaded. "Okay, Adam, have a seat and I'll tell you the basics."

Sitting heavily on Jack's bed, Adam paid close attention while this expert explained the safe handling of a lethal weapon.

Crossing his arms over his chest in frustration, Jack stared at Mark.

"Jack," Mark whispered, "sit down. Please."

"I don't know what good it'll do." Jack made himself comfortable on the couch.

Mark sat next to him.

Jack knew he was waiting for some eye contact, but Jack didn't give him any.

"You think I don't know how much I hurt you."

Jack turned his face away in a blatantly obvious gesture.

"For almost twenty years you have been my best friend. You were the rock I clung to throughout my college life and beyond." Mark reached to touch Jack's leg. When Jack glared at him, he pulled back. "When Dad died, you were there. When I struggled with my studies in class, you were there."

Listening, trying to be strong, Jack heard Mark choke up with emotion and peeked over at him.

"I did want you back then. I wanted all of you. Especially when we were in the dorm room together. I swear, Jack, I thought of going into your bedroom every night. I did. But I was terrified. All my life Dad pegged me as gay, and you know how brutal he was about it." Mark wiped at a tear. "So, I tried to find a woman to hide behind. You knew everything I went through. I held no secrets from you back then. Remember our long chats? We talked about everything."

"I remember."

"I was lost in those days. I was so confused, feeling so much pressure. Not just about my sexuality, but about work. You have any idea how much Dad wanted me to take over Richfield Enterprises? I despised the man. I wouldn't do it."

"I remember that as well." Jack finally met Mark's watery green eyes.

"Then he dies of a bloody stroke and the guilt nearly gutted me. You know Mum blamed me? You know that?"

"No."

"She did. She said I was responsible because I was such a disappointment to him." Mark paused, wiping his face. "So I figured I had to marry Sharon. That I was under some obligation to get an heir and get everyone off my back. It wasn't just Dad's pressure; Mum did her part, believe me."

"I know. Leslie was very strong willed."

"Oh, not half. She was a monster in the guise of a little old lady."

"I know." Jack smiled sadly.

"And by then, Jack, you were the brother I never had. I'm not saying that as some kind of excuse. But I felt so close to you, like I was related to you. It was as if sex with you would either ruin the closeness we had as best friends, or create an intensity I couldn't deal with. I'm not stable. You know that better than most. The fear I had of you becoming my everything—my soul, my brain, and my body—terrified me. You already had all of me, except me physically. And allowing us to go that one step closer made me feel as though I would lose myself, my identity to you. Does this make any sense?"

"In a Mark Richfield sort of way, yes." Jack noticed Mark was opening and closing his hand nervously. Unable to resist, Jack held it still.

"The attraction was there, Jack. It had been there since I set eyes on you in that Stanford baseball uniform. It's still here. It's never gone away. But I kept hoping you would see the reason for my reluctance. I loved you too much. I feel in control with Steve. He's not you. He doesn't have that hold on my soul that you do. I know it should be the reverse, that I should be with you because you do own it, but I can't. I can't allow that last piece of me to flow into you."

When Mark began sobbing, Jack felt his heart break.

Taking a moment to control himself, Mark continued through jerking breaths. "You are my blood. You are my brother. And believe me, in some ways, that's so much closer than Steve and I will ever be. Relationships sometimes come and go, but blood, family, that's forever. With you around, I wasn't an only child. I had a sibling to watch over me. And I'll always be grateful to you."

Reaching out, Jack dabbed at a tear that rolled down Mark's cheek.

"But now, with you rejecting me, and perfectly within your rights to do so, to feel betrayed, to hate me, I can't survive. I am selfish. Yes. I am. You know that as well. I wish I could say it's from a spoilt youth, but that would be a lie. It's from a deprived youth. Maybe because of it I crave your companionship, your love." Mark inhaled deeply. "I feel such a deep hole in my heart without you, I'm always feeling as if I'm ill, or missing something. And I am, love. I'm missing you. Please. I will get down on my knees to beg your forgiveness. Please, Jack. Don't cut me out of your life. Remember our past, our closeness, and find some forgiveness in your heart for a man who is truly lost, and may never feel whole."

Cupping Mark's beautiful feline features, the dampness of his tears wetting Jack's palm, Jack whispered three words he never thought he would ever say to Mark. "I forgive you."

Reaching out to embrace Jack, Mark wailed with relief.

Rubbing his back gently, Jack thought maybe it was time the war was over.

"Repeat the rules to me," Steve requested, a teacher to his student.

"Ah, the gun is always loaded."

Steve nodded.

"Don't put your finger on the trigger unless you are on target and ready to use it." Adam struggled, adding, "Always point the gun in a safe direction. Uh…"

"And be aware of your background."

"Right! Be aware of your background." Adam nodded.

"Okay. Show me the stance again."

Adam steadied his body by placing his legs in a lunge position. With his hands empty, he cupped an imaginary gun and brought his arms up to eye level.

"Good." Steve nudged him as if to see how firm his balance was. "We have to go to a shooting range so you can feel the recoil."

"Okay."

"You more comfortable now?"

"Yes. A lot more comfortable. Thanks."

"Let's see what Mark is doing to poor Jack, shall we?"

"Probably a bloodbath by now." Adam followed him out of the room.

"I don't hear any yelling." Steve descended the stairs.

"Maybe Jack locked him outside."

They stepped into the living room and found Mark sobbing on Jack's shoulder. "Huh," he said to Steve. "Could this be a reconciliation?"

"It's long fucking overdue," Steve replied.

As if he had heard them talking, Jack looked up and caught their gazes. He tapped Mark, who sat up, wiping his eyes.

"Hello, gents." Mark tried to smile and pretend things were okay. "Just reminiscing about old times, you know."

"Sure, Mark," Steve replied, "Just tell me you guys have finally formed a damn truce."

"We have." Jack reached for Adam.

Hurrying over, Adam held his hand, and was directed to sit on Jack's lap. Wrapping his arms around Jack's neck, Adam stared at Mark, curious as to what his reaction would be to their cuddle.

Mark smiled sweetly. "You have a good one there, Adam. Take care of him."

"No shit. You don't think I know that?"

Steve sat down on the floor in front of Mark. "You guys work it out?"

"Yes." Jack tightened his grip around Adam's waist.

"Thank fuck!" Steve shouted. "I was sick to death of the whining."

"I don't whine. Don't be rude." Mark kept dabbing at his eyes like he were a woman whose make-up was smeared.

Adam couldn't get over him. "You know, you'd make the perfect actor. Looks and emotion. Want me to list you with my agency?"

"Don't swell his head anymore than it already is." Steve leaned against Mark's lap.

"No, Mr. Lewis. I've had enough offers on that account. I don't want to be an actor or a model."

"He did act in a play," Jack informed them.

"Oh, don't bring that up!" Mark rolled his eyes.

"No!" Steve sat back. "You did? A play?"

Adam was enjoying this group immensely, not to mention the warmth of Jack's lap under him. There was a tenderness to these men he enjoyed. They were good company and they all seemed to share some common ground.

"Oh, Jack, why did you bring that up?" Mark groaned.

"Because you were awesome in it."

"Come on!" Steve prodded. "Now you have to tell us!"

"He played Eliza Doolittle in an all male gay version of *My Fair Lady*." Jack grinned broadly.

Adam became hysterical with laughter while Steve rolled on the floor holding his stomach.

"Thanks, Jackie. Now I'll never hear the end of it." Mark sighed.

"I don't know what you have to be ashamed of Mark. It was a great play," Jack replied.

"Eliza Doolittle?" Steve tried to control himself and sat back up over Mark's lap. "Did you kiss Henry Higgins?"

"No, but that actor who played Freddy Eynsford-Hill planted one on me. Totally unscripted. It was embarrassing." Mark caressed the back of Steve's head.

"And..." Jack urged Mark to continue.

"And? Oh, you don't need me to go into that as well," Mark complained.

Adam was enthralled, envisioning the play in his head, again thinking big film possibilities. Or in reality, maybe a small underground theater instead.

Jack nudged Mark. "Go on, tell them."

"Fine! It seems Mr. Larsen doesn't want any stone left unturned on this tale." Mark ran his hand back through his hair. "Well, there's a part in the play where Eliza first comes over to Henry Higgins' house in need of lessons. And she gets stripped by the maids for a bath."

Adam's eyes grew wide. "No way."

"Yes, way." Mark nodded. "The lights were supposed to go out right as they stripped me from the waist down, and I was supposed to cover myself up at that second."

Jack grinned. "They fucked up the timing."

"I was bloody exposed on the flamin' stage for a split second!" Mark explained, "My bleedin' Mum was in the audience. I was mortified."

"Made the whole damn show. Everyone was talking about it at intermission." Jack started chuckling.

"That is absolutely hilarious," Adam said. "Do you have that play on tape?"

"No! And if I did, I'd burn it." Mark tried to draw Steve closer. Steve moved to lie across Mark's lap.

"Oh," Jack said, "speaking about tapes, Mark, do you know where that copy of *Lust* is?"

"That Plimpton porn film?" Mark asked. "Why?"

"*Lust?*" Steve sat up eagerly. "Gay porn?"

"Don't tell me you've never heard of Buster Plimpton?" Mark gaped at him.

"Wait a minute." Steve held up his finger for them to give him a second. "Yes. Loveday. I met him in Redondo at a bookshop. We had a drink together. It was right before Mark decided to end his relationship with Sharon. I was trying to keep away from this Brit. But good ole Mark showed up at the hotel anyway."

Adam said, "I remember those movies. Plimpton directed Loveday in some pretty racy Eighties cult films."

Steve seemed to drift off.

"What made you think of that video, Jackie?" Mark asked.

"When Adam and I went out to dinner on the pier in Redondo, someone had stapled a nude photo of Loveday to a tree."

"Ouch." Mark shivered. "Bet he'd be upset with that. I know I would."

"Where is it? Do I have it or did you take it with you when you moved out?"

"I didn't take it. You must have it."

"Get it! Play it!" Steve shouted. "I love those old movies and haven't watched them in ages. Christ, I didn't think any of the copies were around anymore."

Adam laughed. "Great, four horny gay guys watching porn together."

143

"Can you think of anything better to do?" Mark asked.

"I'll go look for it." Jack tapped Adam to get off his lap.

"I'll order pizza!" Steve jumped to his feet.

After Jack and Steve vanished, Adam sat next to Mark on the couch. "Are you guys really okay?"

"Yes. Thank you for asking, Adam."

"I just want the tension to be gone. Jack's got enough to worry about with my case and work."

"I agree. How are things going with you? Can you talk about it?"

"I don't know. I think it'll be all right."

"If I may ask, why do you need instructions in using a gun?"

Opening his mouth to respond, Adam closed it again. In reality, he didn't know the answer to that question.

Before he was able to come up with a plausible comment, Jack entered the room, waving a VHS tape in his hand. "Found it."

From the other room, Steve shouted, "Everything but anchovies?"

"Yes!" they replied.

"Don't you dare start it without me!" Steve yelled.

"We won't!" Mark answered back.

"Can I see it?" Adam allowed Jack back his place on the sofa and sat on his lap once more. Reading the cover of the plastic box, seeing the cheesy Eighties design, Adam asked. "You have any idea how many times I've jerked off to this one?"

Mark's laughter filled the room. Seconds later, Steve came racing in. "Pizza's on its way. Ya got beer?"

"In the fridge."

"Is that it?" Steve gestured to the tape. Adam handed it to him, watching his reaction.

"Wow!" Steve gushed. "You know when I met him in person I thought Mark was prettier than he was. But seeing how he looks in these films, Loveday is better looking than you, Mark."

"You think?" Mark winked at Adam teasingly.

"How do you like that, boys? I finally found a man on the planet to put Mark Antonious' beauty to the test." Steve handed Jack the tape. "Four beers?" he hollered as he walked away.

"Yes!" they replied in unison.

"Mark Antonious?" Adam taunted.

"Yes. Don't you start. I've had enough stick over that name."

"Stick?" Adam asked.

"Teasing!" Mark clarified.

"Put it in the VCR." Jack handed the tape to Mark.

While Mark crouched in front of the VCR, Adam mouthed silently to Jack, "Mark Antonious?"

Grinning slyly, Jack indicated not to torment Mark about it.

Steve showed up, a beer in each hand. "Here's two."

Jack and Adam took one each as Steve raced to get the others. "Don't you dare start that without me!" Sprinting, returning with two more iced mugs of beer in his hands, Steve waited for Mark to sit down on the couch. Once he handed him his drink, Steve sat in front of him on the floor, leaning back on Mark's legs. "Start it. Come on!"

"Before the pizza guy gets here?" Adam asked, his mug of beer near his lips.

"Yeah, we'll pause it." Steve reached for the remote that had ended up in Mark's hand.

"I just hope the poor pizza guy doesn't come in to find two gay couples humping on the living room floor." Adam reclined back on Jack's chest as Steve hit the play button.

The room going quiet, Jack reached for the light switch on a standing lamp and made the room darker. The opening credits began along with the dated soundtrack. Those weren't the days of personal computers and cell phones, more like eight-tracks and disco.

As the movie scene began, Adam couldn't resist a peek at Steve. He seemed like a kid about to go on a field trip to a toy store. His blue eyes were wide and the beer glass was in his mouth like a sucker.

Focusing back on the screen, Adam felt Jack's light caress on his arm and watched the action on the tube. Within the first few moments, the sex scenes had already begun.

A back alley, money being exchanged, Angel Loveday is on his knees in front of a customer, sucking the man's large dick. It's an undercover sting. The customer is a cop, but he still wants this macho stud to suck him. It's only after the cop has come in Angel's mouth that he flashes his badge and tells him he's under arrest. Five men in uniform materialize from all over the alley. Angel is placed against a graffiti-covered brick wall. Three stunningly handsome officers feel every part of Angel's body up simultaneously; inside his trademark tight, torn, faded, blue jeans, up his naked torso, through his hair. The look of ecstasy on Angel's face is phenomenal. A deal is struck. Lots of butt fucking and cock sucking on Angel's part and he gets off with just a warning.

Steve hissed, "I'm a cop and I've never done that to anyone."

"Oh, yeah?" Mark challenged.

"I mean, on the job, duh!"

"You think Loveday still acts?" Adam asked Jack.

"I don't know. I haven't seen him in anything lately."

"Wonder what he looks like now?" Adam mused.

"Ask Steve. He's the one who met him recently."

"Shh! Oh, Christ, he's fucking gorgeous!" Steve hushed them.

"Later," Adam whispered, "he's too enthralled."

They all got back to watching the movie until the doorbell interrupted them with their dinner. Mark reluctantly stopped the movie. One by one they stood up to get ready for dinner.

After they were sitting at the table Adam asked Steve, "So? What's Loveday look like now?"

"Fucking gorgeous." Steve seemed to be inhaling his food.

Chewing his slice of pizza, Adam said, "Slow down, Steve. You'll choke!"

"I want to watch the rest of it. Man, how come you guys never told me you had his videos? Jesus, Mark, you knew about them and kept them from me?"

"Kept them from you?" Mark nibbled his pizza slice. "What? Were he and I secret lovers? Aren't you being a bit silly? Besides, it's you that's kept him from me. You never even mentioned you had a drink with him."

"I know. Sorry. It was during the period of insanity right before you were about to marry Sharon. Never mind." Steve finished his slice of pizza. "I had no idea you guys had his old videos. You know how much shit like this turns me on. I'm a sucker for all you pretty boys." Steve gulped his beer.

"Then don't become an agent," Adam warned. "You'll lose your mind."

"No, not all guys do it for me." Steve wiped his mouth with his napkin. "Just the long-haired ones with the androgynous faces and big dicks."

"That counts me out," Adam laughed.

"Me, too." Jack picked up another pizza slice.

"I suppose you're all staring at me for some reason?" Mark asked in annoyance.

Steve winked at Jack. "Nah, you don't fit that description. Not much." He brushed off his hands. "Come on! I want to get back in there to see the rest of the film!"

"Go!" Mark waved at him.

"We should have just eaten in the living room," Adam suggested.

Instantly Steve picked up the pizza box and carried it into the other room.

Mark leaned over to whisper, "You believe him? He's smitten!"

"Well, Angel Loveday," Jack replied, as if it was obvious.

147

Adam smiled. "I think it's adorable."

"Me, too," Mark giggled.

"Come on!" Steve thundered from the other room.

"Coming!" Mark answered. "Or I will be shortly."

Adam looked over at Jack, glad to see his smile.

Chapter Ten

Jack Turner fidgeted in the chair nervously. His defense attorney, the DA, the prosecutor, and the detective on the case were all staring at him as if he were a vile creature.

"As you know, Mr. Turner," DA Aiden began, "a new witness has come forward to testify against you. And since that witness showed up, two more have approached our office."

"Two more?" Turner asked. "Who? What are their names?"

"We can't divulge that at this time. But believe me, Mr. Turner, they hold or held contracts with your agency, and are very credible witnesses."

"I thought the accused has a right to face his accuser! Arthur! Aren't you going to say something?"

Arthur asked, "Will we get a list of witnesses that the prosecutor is calling to the stand?"

"You will, but in exchange for their testimony, they have requested protection, so their names will be blacked out."

"This is bullshit!" Turner shouted. "I don't get why this is such a big deal? Don't you idiots know anything about show business? You think I'm the only one who has these couch practices?"

"Turner!" Arthur shouted. "You're incriminating yourself!"

"No I ain't! I'm lettin' these morons know it's done!

They just decided to single me out. Right? Did Logan offer someone in here sex just because he couldn't pass an audition?"

"That's quite enough, Mr. Turner," DA Aiden chided. "Your lawyer has offered you our terms. You can either accept them, plead guilty and go to jail for your crimes, or go to trial."

"I ain't pleadin' guilty to shit. Get me outa here. This is a waste of my fricken time."

Arthur waited until his client had stormed out. "I think he wants a trial."

"That's fine, Mr. Harris."

Turner stood outside the doorway, wringing his hands. Turner asked, "What's our next option?"

"Trial. We don't have any other options." Arthur escorted them to the elevator.

"Trial." Turner echoed.

When they were on street level in front of the courthouse, Turner shouted at his defense attorney, "If you think I'm going to let those mongrels put me on trial and send me to jail, you're insane."

"What are you going to do?"

"None of your fucking business. But I am going to do something."

Adam leaned over Natalie's shoulder while she added more information to the calendar on the computer. "Right...this week, what have we got that I need to be aware of?"

"Everyone is cool, except Logan. He wants you with him for the meeting with that movie producer. Freeman?"

"Yes. Tomorrow at ten? Am I picking him up?"

"You decide. You want a driver to get him and meet him at the producer's office?"

"Yes. Thanks. That way we don't have to hang out together after. I'll just get him the script and he can go home."

"Okay, Adam."

"Thanks, Natalie."

Adam took his mobile phone out of his pocket. When Jack answered, Adam asked, "Jack? Can you talk?"

"Yeah, what's up?"

Moving to the hall, Adam whispered, "Steve's taking me to that shooting range tomorrow."

"Good. What time?"

"During his lunch break. I have a quick meeting in the morning, then I'm joining him there."

"You're carrying it on you now, right? I got you your permit."

"Jack…" Adam heard Natalie telling Logan about the driver and car. He moved further out of her hearing range. "I'd prefer just keeping it in my trunk, unloaded."

"No! You wear the fucking thing!"

Blinking in surprise at Jack's tenacity, Adam nodded mechanically. "All right, but I still haven't even fired it. I thought I'd wait until Steve showed me how—"

"Adam!"

"Jack? What's going on? Why are you being so adamant about this?"

A deep exhale of Jack's breath preceded his comment. "I got a call from the DA."

"And?"

"Two more victims have come forward."

"That's good news, isn't it?" Adam peered back and found Natalie typing again.

"Yes. But DA Aiden told me they had a meeting with Turner and his lawyer. She said Turner was highly agitated and threatening."

Adam swallowed nervously. "Why didn't they hold him?"

"He didn't break the law. He was just a little unstable."

"But that's Turner. He's always that way."

"Adam." Jack's voice grew more forceful.

"Okay, Jack. I'll wear it. I just won't feel comfortable until Steve shoots with me at the range."

"I don't care."

"I've got to go. So, see you at your place to work out later?"

"Yes. Please, be careful."

"I will." Adam hung up, reentering the room where Natalie was working. Standing at one of the windows that faced the front of the house, Adam felt his nerves kick in at the thought of Turner seeking revenge.

"You okay, Adam?"

"Hmm? Yes. Nothing you have to worry about, Natalie."

"Logan will meet you in front of Freeman's building at ten to ten."

"Perfect. You're a doll. Which driver did you call?"

"Uh, it was listed in your telephone directory. Black Stretch?"

"Oh."

"Was that not the right one to get? I can phone back."

"No. No, it should be okay." Adam knew that was the service Turner used most. He didn't think there would being any chance of a problem, Adam sighed. "No big deal, Natalie."

When she smiled and picked the phone back up, he moved his gaze to the dresser's top drawer. Inside it lay a revolver in a waist-pack holster and a box of bullets.

Chapter Eleven

Mark watched as Steve clipped a shoulder holster around him to conceal under his suit jacket. Once it was secure, Steve checked that his Glock was loaded, then slid it into the leather, snapping it in place. As he put his jacket over the top of it, Mark said, "When was the last time you wore that thing?"

"Off duty, when I was still a cop." Steve adjusted his clothing, straightening himself out.

"I don't like it."

"I don't really like it either anymore. I've gotten used to not carrying it. And besides, I have you to protect me now." Steve grinned and got into a boxing stance.

"Ha ha." Mark wasn't amused.

"I want to show Adam how to shoot. It's one hour, Mark."

"Just be careful. Don't go saving any banks from robbers or anything."

"Yes, dear." Steve kissed him. "You meeting Jack for lunch?"

"No. We decided we'd all get together for dinner instead. He found another Loveday film. *Filth*."

"Oh, yes! I love that guy. Those movies are fantastic. He's my new idol. And, man, was the sex hot that night or what?" Steve wrapped his arm around Mark's waist, drawing him close.

"It's always hot, copper." When Steve gave Mark a long wet lick on the face, Mark peeked out of their office window. "Behave. We're at work."

"See ya in an hour." Steve headed to the door.

"Please be careful." As Steve waved goodbye, Mark felt an unpleasant pang of nerves in his gut.

Adam stood with Logan out in front of the producer's office building, the phone to his ear. "Hello? Steve? I'm just finishing my meeting. Are you already at the range?"

"No. I'm in my car and on my way. Where are you? Where's the office building?"

"Right off Sunset Boulevard. Why? Are you close?"

"Yes, really close. I can swing by and get you. No point in taking two cars."

"You sure? You have to get back to work after."

"But I'll pass by the building on my way. Let me pick you up."

"Okay." Adam hung up, turning his attention to Logan. "Right, you have your script, read it through and tell me if you're interested."

"I'm already interested, Adam." Logan smiled shyly. "I can't believe you got me such a good offer."

"I know. Just make it look as though you're not eager." Adam checked the area for Logan's chauffeur. Glancing at his watch, Adam mumbled, "Where is he? I thought he'd hang out here and just wait for you. Let me get something out of my car, someone is picking me up."

"Okay, Adam."

Adam took his keys out of his pocket, walked to his car, and opened his trunk. Picking up the heavy waist-pack, he was reluctant to wrap it around his hips while wearing his best silk suit. He held it in his hand, closed his trunk, chirped the alarm on his car, and headed back to where Logan stood. A distinct crack of a gunshot sounded. Adam ducked in reflex and watched Logan drop down to the sidewalk. For a minute Adam assumed Logan was just hitting the deck to hide from the noise, then he realized that was not the case. "Logan!"

A roaring, revving engine noise startled him as he ran towards the fallen man. A gold Cadillac hopped the curb, resting sideways over the sidewalk and an arm with a gun poked out.

"Holy shit!"

A bullet whizzed over Adam's head. Adam hid behind a car and called 911 frantically. As he dialed and was connected, an ear-shatteringly loud blast with glass breaking and metal crunching scared the crap out of him. Taking a look over the hood he was crouching behind, he found a car had crashed into Turner's. In terror, Adam realized Steve Miller had hit the Cadillac with his own car and now stood over its driver, pointing the gun at his head.

"Oh, my fucking god! Hello? Police! Help! Someone just shot a friend of mine and an ex-LAPD cop is holding the armed suspect at gun point! We're on Sunset Boulevard! Oh, Christ, hurry!"

A voice ordered, "Don't move! Drop the gun!"

Adam heard Steve's commands. Turner still had his gun? And Steve was risking his life? Finally remembering his own weapon, Adam struggled with shaking hands to open the zipper, pulling it out and holding the grip of the heavy pistol in his hand. His entire body trembling, he moved slowly to get over to Logan, terrified for Logan's life. Pointing the gun away from himself awkwardly, he crouched down and was relieved Logan was breathing. "Hang in there. I've called for help."

"Drop it or I'll shoot!" Steve ordered in a militaristic way, both his hands poised on the butt of the gun, his finger on the trigger. His car was smoking and hissing from the collision he caused.

Blood seeped through Logan's shirt. Adam looked behind him, hoping Steve had some control over Turner because both he and Logan were in the line of fire. Adam peeled back Logan's fingers to see the damage. A black hole punctured the right side of his chest under his collar bone. Taking off his suit jacket, Adam used the material to push against the wound to stop the bleeding. "Hurry, you fucking police!"

A blast sounded. Adam shouted in fear and jumped up. He was out of his mind worrying about Steve. Seeing Steve still standing, his gun still pointed, Adam told Logan, "I'll be right back, hold on."

Racing to Steve's side, Adam found Steve's vision fixed on Turner's body as the fiend slumped over the steering wheel.

"You shot him?"

"He...he shot himself."

Seeing Steve's lack of a physical reaction, Adam lowered Steve's arms slowly. "Okay, Steve. He's dead. You can put the gun down."

"Did you call the police?"

As Steve said it, Adam heard the sirens approaching from all sides.

"Steve, are you okay? Logan's been hit by a bullet."

"What?" Steve jerked his head around and went running. They both crouched down beside Logan.

"Logan?" Adam whispered. "The ambulance is on its way. Hold on."

Logan nodded but was growing pale.

Steve moved Adam's jacket aside and looked at the wound. "At least it's not near his heart. But the exit wound will be worse than the entry." Steve rolled Logan over slowly, sliding the jacket under his shoulder where most of the blood flowed. "You okay, Logan?"

"When's the ambulance coming?"

Adam stood up. "The cops are here." He ran to them waving. "We have a man shot!" They nodded, shouting for the medics.

Crouching down with Steve to encourage Logan to hold on, the fire crew finally set their kits down and took over.

As they did, Steve picked up the handgun Adam had left near Logan and handed it back to him.

Adam took it reluctantly. "Lot of good I did."

"Don't worry. I took care of it."

"What would I have done if you hadn't come by?"

"Don't worry about it." Steve wrapped his arm around Adam's waist. They walked with the gurney that held Logan to be loaded on an ambulance.

"Call my partner," Logan said as he was wheeled by.

Adam hurried to his side, writing down Logan's partner's phone number on his hand as Logan recited it. "I got it."

Taking out his phone, Adam became aware of a crowd of officers around Steve as he recounted the events. When the line connected, Adam said, "Yes, hello, George? This is Adam Lewis, Logan's agent. He's been involved in a shooting and is being transported to the emergency room." As he filled Logan's terrified partner in on the details, Adam noticed Steve's smile as he was reunited with some his old comrades in arms. Once Adam had finished with his call, he walked over to the smashed Caddy to stare at the corpse of Jack Turner. A hole had been blown through the back of his head from where he had swallowed the barrel of the gun. Blood spattered the back seat's leather interior. "Nice one, Turner. This was your solution? Kill me and Logan and then yourself?"

A warm hand caressed his back. Seeing Steve's reassuring smile, Adam felt better.

"Look at it this way, Adam. No trial. No humiliation. Just a funeral."

"I still can't help but feel sad. I worked with the guy for a decade."

"You have too much sympathy for him, Adam. He was a sick fucker who abused too many men in his lifetime."

Nodding, Adam said, "You're right. I know."

Adam's phone rang. He took it out of his pocket. "Hello?"

157

G.A. Hauser

"Hiya, babe. How's the training going at the range?"

Staring at the wrecked automobiles, the dozen patrol cars and milling cops and media, Adam didn't know where to begin.

"Adam? You there? Are you outside the range?"

"We never made it to the range, Jack."

"Why? Oh, no. What happened?"

Looking back at Steve who was busy answering more questions from uniformed men with bars and stripes on their sleeves, Adam replied, "It's a long story, Jack. Can I just come and see you?"

"Yes. Are you all right?"

"I'm fine. We're fine."

"You want to come to my office or do you want to meet me home?"

"At your home. I may be a little while."

"Adam! At least give me a hint! Did you have an accident at the range?"

"Turner shot himself in the head. He's dead."

"What? How do you know? Did someone call you about it?"

"No. He did it in front of us. Look, get a bottle of strong booze. Both Steve and I are going to need it."

"Should I call Mark?"

Glancing over again at Steve, seeing him on his mobile phone, Adam said, "I think Steve is doing that right now."

"Okay, Adam. I'll wait until you get here. But are you sure you're all right?"

"Yes. Steve and I are fine."

"Okay. See you soon."

"See you soon." Adam shut off his phone. Glancing back at the entrance of the office building where Logan had fallen, the occupants of the office had come down to gawk. Seeing his bloody jacket lying there, Adam went to retrieve it, wishing he felt relief and not nausea.

158

Driving Steve to Jack's place, Adam kept glancing over at his profile, seeing Steve's exhaustion clearly on his face. "While you were a cop, did you ever shoot anyone?"

"No."

"I'm sorry you had to go through that on my account."

"Will you stop apologizing? I didn't have to shoot the guy. And it wasn't your fault. I'm just glad I was there or you could have been hurt."

Or dead. Adam shivered.

When he pulled into Jack's driveway, both Mark and Jack were waiting at the door. Adam shut the car off, and he and Steve climbed out. Jack rushed out to embrace Adam as Mark did the same to Steve.

"Come on, let's get inside." Jack held Adam's hand and escorted them in.

Steve kept reassuring Mark he was okay. Mark was hysterical over the incident, holding onto Steve with a vice-like grip.

Tossing his gun pack down on a side table, Adam loosened his tie and kicked off his shoes as Jack began passing out shots of whiskey. Dropping down on the sofa, Adam shot it down and shivered with the after burn. Steve did the same, collapsing on a chair and letting out a long low breath.

Mark climbed onto Steve's lap nuzzling him.

Jack joined Adam on the couch. "So? Turner shot Logan and then himself?"

"Yes. Jack, it was terrifying." Adam handed him the glass. "One more?"

Jack retrieved the bottle.

"My hero," Mark moaned, kissing Steve's face.

"No kidding!" Adam agreed taking the full glass from Jack as he sat down again. "I'd be dead without you, Steve. You are unreal."

"I suppose my cop instinct kicked in. I drove up and saw Turner's arm out of that window pointing the gun. Then I saw the two of you standing in his sites. I couldn't fucking believe it. I figured if I hit him with the car, at least I'd shake him up for his next shot."

"Oh, my poor baby," Mark cooed, wrapping around him.

Steve continued, "And it worked. When I jumped out of the car he must have been in shock. Maybe he hit his head or something. He didn't have his seatbelt on and the airbag didn't deploy. I figure he got his noggin knocked." Mark reached for the whiskey and poured Steve another shot. "Thanks, babe. Anyway, so I got out and pointed my gun at him, ordering him to drop his. He didn't. He didn't point it at me. He just sat with it in his hand. I figure he must have thought I was an off duty cop and the jig was up."

Adam listened to Steve's portion of the story. He figured on what had happened, but it was amazing hearing Steve tell it.

"Then he starts moving the gun. I began pulling back the trigger thinking he was going to try and shoot me before I shot him. Then, really slowly, he puts the fucking barrel in his mouth."

Mark cringed and closed his eyes.

"I still screamed at him to drop the gun, but I knew by then it was over." Steve belted down the second shot. "It was sick watching it though. The stuff of nightmares. Christ." He shivered in exaggeration.

Adam noticed Jack gazing at him. Adam shrugged. "I was just standing there with Logan when we heard shots. I think I had just walked over to get my gun out of my car."

"Out of your car?" Jack interrupted.

"Jack, please."

"I warned you." Jack pointed his finger at Adam.

"Anyway!" Adam held up his hand to be allowed to continue. "When I shut my trunk I heard the blast. I thought Logan was just ducking like I was. I didn't even realize the shots were aimed our way. I just figured we were near some gang shooting thing. It wasn't until I recognized Turner's Caddy that I figured it out, and then of course I found out Logan was shot."

"Is he okay?" Jack asked.

"Yes, thank God. He's just been hit in the upper chest area. It went straight through. Nothing was damaged but muscle tissue. Christ, he's lucky."

Jack addressed Steve. "What happens now with you?"

"Nothing. Maybe more questions after the autopsy, but it was obviously self-inflicted. It's got nothing to do with me."

"Even ramming his car?" Jack asked.

"Yes, Mr. Attorney, even ramming his car. The lieutenant on the scene was one of my old co-workers, Gary. Believe me, he's not even going to make the insurance companies argue. It was all on Turner. I was saving lives."

"Good. Because you know I'm here if you need me."

"Nope, ding dong the witch is dead." Steve nudged Mark for another refill.

Jack said, "Oh, Steve, an old friend of yours on the department, Isaac Johnson wants you to call him to get together for a beer. We met when Adam had to call the cops last week."

"Okay, thanks, Jack."

"I had a bad feeling when you left the office, Steve." Mark poured more booze for him, resting the bottle down again on the coffee table. "You know how you get those feelings?"

"Woman's intuition?" Jack teased.

"Shut up, He-man."

"I need a shower." Adam placed his empty glass down.

"Ditto. And a nap. I'm really out of it." Steve plopped his glass down as well.

"Oh, do we have to go? I don't want to go." Mark pouted his bottom lip.

"You're welcome to stay," Jack offered.

"No, thanks, Jack. I don't have any clean clothing with me." Steve stretched his back. "Come on, Mr. Richfield, drive me home in your fancy TVR."

"Okay, if you insist." Mark held his hand. "Bye, Jackie, Adam. I'm glad you're all right."

"Thanks, Mark."

"Can we come by soon? See that other Loveday film?" Mark asked.

"Sure." Jack walked him to the door.

"Yes! Another Loveday film? Really?" Steve lit up.

"Yes, dear. He made dozens of them," Mark hugged him.

"You made my day!"

Adam waved and shouted, "Thanks again, Steve."

"No problem." Steve waved back.

When Jack closed the door, it was dead silent in the house. Adam stared at him.

Slowly Jack turned to face him. "Are you okay?"

"I'm shaken up. But yes, I'm okay."

Moving closer, Jack rubbed Adam's shoulders gently. "Come on, I'll draw you a hot bubble bath."

"Join me?"

"You bet."

"Ooh la la!" Adam allowed Jack to maneuver him up the stairs to the bedroom.

Taking off his clothing as Jack started the water running in the tub, Adam caught his own reflection in the mirror. He appeared slightly ragged, but after the experience he just had, he assumed it was expected. Once he had removed his upper half of clothing, he stepped closer to that image in the glass and ran his hand through his hair. "If I hadn't have met Jack, I wouldn't have met Steve, and I'd be dead right now."

"Sorry?" Jack asked, standing near the bathroom door. "Did you say something?"

"Talking to myself." Adam stepped out of his suit trousers, dropping them in a pile on the floor. "I suppose I should toss those. The jacket was so full of Logan's blood I threw it out."

"I'll buy you a new suit."

162

"Oh, Jack." Adam yawned, showing his weariness.

"Come here, baby." Jack picked him up and carried him to the waiting tub. The scent of spicy cinnamon bubble-bath in the air, Jack lowered Adam into the water slowly.

Letting out an audible sigh, Adam closed his eyes and sank into the white foam. Jack disrobed beside the tub, cupping his balls, stepping in gingerly.

"Too hot for you?" Adam's laugh echoed off the tiled walls.

"Just getting used to it. Ah!"

"I love it. The hotter the better." Adam sank lower, groaning.

Once Jack had acclimated his body to the heat, he found Adam's leg under the suds and began rubbing soap on it, washing him.

"You spoil me."

"You need spoiling."

Blinking his eyes open, Adam found that the worried expression remained on Jack's fine features. "I'm okay, Jack."

"I know."

"And can we safely say it's over?"

"Yes. We can safely say it's over." Jack lowered Adam's left leg, picking his right one out of the water to wash. "I have one question about what happened."

"Please, not about me and the gun."

"No. Not about that."

"What then?"

"How did Turner know you and Logan would be at that office building at that time? What were the odds of him just randomly driving by and seeing you?"

"Oh. I have a theory on that one that I am going to investigate tomorrow."

"I'd like to hear it."

"When I asked Natalie to get a limo for Logan, she used the one from my personal directory book. Black Stretch. Turner's favorite company. I have a feeling he asked some

163

of his buddies there to keep an ear out for any of our appointments. My guess is that our driver let Turner know."

"Conspiracy?"

"No. Most likely Turner made up some story. I doubt the chauffeur had a clue."

"Makes sense." Jack allowed Adam's leg to slide back under water. Sitting up, Jack began washing Adam's chest and shoulders.

"Spoiled, spoiled, spoiled…" Adam moaned, closing his eyes.

A low chuckle came from Jack.

Chapter Twelve

Almost as if the ghost of Jack Turner was lurking around a corner, Adam walked into his posh downtown office warily.

The office they shared, the one they had worked in for the last ten years before the allegations of sexual assault surfaced. Pocketing his key, Adam looked around. The place seemed like a vacuum with no employees inhabiting it. Walking from room to room, Natalie behind him eyeing the photos of their popular clients on the walls, Adam wondered if he could move in, or if he would feel too much of the looming presence that Turner left behind.

Entering Turner's private office, Adam immediately turned to look at the "couch". The infamous couch that Jack Turner had conducted his "business" on. "I'm going to burn that thing." Adam shivered in disgust. Crossing the carpet to the large dark mahogany desk, Adam read the paperwork curiously. It seemed as if Turner hadn't been back to this office in months either. The dates on the letters were old. Sitting down in the chair, swiveling it, Adam heard his name being called. "In here, Natalie."

She poked her head in. "Wow. Fancy."

"What do you think? Should we stay here or move?"

"Up to you. But I like it. It's really done up nice. And it looks so new."

"Where do you want your desk?"

"Out there." She pointed. "Right outside this office."

"My old desk." Adam smiled.

"Oh, is that okay?"

"Perfect."

"Wow, look at all those stars," she gushed, staring at the photos.

"I wonder how they'll feel with just me as their agent?"

"Relieved!" she shouted.

"Yes, most likely." He stood and pushed in the chair. "Okay. We'll keep it. Just get rid of that."

She turned to the couch. "Is that where…"

"Yes."

"Yipes. I'll call someone today."

"Good girl." Adam walked out into the lobby with her. "I think we should send out letters to everyone that we're located back here again. Most of our clients figured this place was off limits. Let's get them back on track."

"You got it, Adam."

Adam winked at her and took another look around the place.

Jack had just finished the narration of the incident involving Jack Turner to his staff. "And if it wasn't for Steve's amazing police training, who knows what would have happened."

Jennifer, Sonja, and the rest were silent while they listened to the shocking details.

Finally Jennifer said, "Well, I'm not surprised."

"No?" Sonja asked.

"Turner was a madman. He did what madmen do. At least my client doesn't have to worry about him anymore."

"No." Sonja shook her head. "No one has to worry about that monster anymore."

"Okay," Jennifer moved them on, "what else is on the agenda?"

After the meeting, Jennifer asked Jack confidentially, "How's Adam doing? Is he all right?"

"Yes. He seems to be. He's trying to get the business back on its feet again. He said he was moving back into the downtown office."

"I can take care of the paperwork for him. You know, the transfer of the business license."

"Oh, great. Thanks, Jen."

"Did Turner have any family? Did he leave a will?"

"I have no idea."

"I just thought it would be ironic if he did and left everything to Adam."

"What are the odds?" Jack asked.

Jennifer shrugged. "Stranger things have happened, Jack." She walked away waving her hand in the air. "Stranger things."

With that odd notion in his head, Jack called Adam. "Hey."

"Hey, blondie."

"Ah, Jennifer just asked me an odd question."

"Yes?"

"Does Turner have any family?"

"Not that I know of. You mean to take care of his funeral?"

"That and his will."

"His will? I have no idea."

"You know who his lawyer is?"

"I think so. He's got him somewhere in his files. Why?"

"I don't know. Maybe you're the beneficiary."

"I don't want a fucking thing from Turner! If I am, I'll turn it over to charity."

"Oh. Good man."

"We getting together with Mark and Steve later?"

"Yes." Jack sat down in his chair in his office. "You okay with that?"

"More than okay. Steve saved my damn life, Jack."

"That's the kind of guy he is," Jack replied, smiling. "Mark's got a good one there. I have to admit."

"Yes. He does. What a fricken hero. I am still impressed

with his performance. I'd like to do something for him. Any idea what he'd like?"

"Mark, tied to a bed?"

"Ha ha. No, really. Think about it."

"I will. See ya later." Jack hung up and smiled contentedly. With Adam's question still on his mind, Jack dialed Mark's cell phone.

"Hullo?"

"Hello, Mr. Richfield."

"Hello, Jackie-blue."

"My lover wants to know how he can thank your lover."

"Oh, believe me, he's been rewarded."

"I have no doubt, but Adam still wants it to come from him, not you."

"I don't know, Jack. But I'll give it some thought and get back to you."

"Great. Thanks, Mark."

"See you tonight?"

"You will." Jack hung up and turned on his computer. As it booted up, he got an idea, then quickly got back on the phone with Adam.

Adam used his key to enter Jack's house. "Hello?"

"I'm in the gym."

"I'll get changed."

"Any luck?"

"I'll be in in a minute." Adam dropped his bag and began changing into his shorts and t-shirt. Once he was ready, he met Jack in the workout room. "I made a few phone calls. I still don't know yet."

"If you can pull that off, Steve would die."

"Hey, I can try." Adam stepped on the treadmill and began his slow warm up.

"So? Are you moving into the old office?"

"Yup!"

"Did Natalie like it?"

"She loved it."

"Good."

Adam smiled to himself as he increased the speed. Could life be good? Could he get this lucky?

Once they were both covered in sweat, Jack sat next to Adam on the mat as he completed his sit-ups. Jack held his feet for him for his last few tough ones. Finally Adam dropped back. "Enough for today."

"You are looking so fit!" Jack rubbed Adam's taut belly roughly.

"Hey, that tickles!" Adam twisted away.

Jack gripped Adam's arms and pinned him down. "I should fuck you right here on the mat."

Feeling Jack jamming his hard-on against him, Adam replied, "You already are, Larsen."

"Not quite." Jack's teeth showed as he struggled to get his hands into Adam's gym shorts.

"Hey! You molesting me?"

"Yes, you got a problem with that?" Jack wrenched Adam's shorts down his hips.

"You think you can do it?" Adam laughed.

"Yes."

"Christ!" Adam struggled to get a grip on his clothing but Jack wasn't allowing him the reach. Suddenly Adam felt Jack's cock poking him. "Larsen! How the hell did you do that so quickly?"

"Hornier than hell." Jack shoved his dick between Adam's legs, rubbing up against him, humping him.

"Wouldn't you rather use a rubber and lube and be in?" Adam asked, looking up at Jack as he arched his back, leaning up over him for good leverage.

"Squeeze."

Adam flexed his legs, clamping Jack between his thighs. Feeling Jack's cock ramming up under his balls, Adam stared at Jack in fascination. "Mark's right, you are a brute."

169

Stifling a chuckle, Jack said, "Shut up, I'm almost there." After some more pumping, Jack ordered, "Tighter."

"Jack! I'll get a cramp I'm squeezing your dick so tight. Let's go upstairs and—"

"Ah! Ah!"

Adam shut up. Hot come blasted against his ass and slid down his crack as he lay back. "I've been manhandled. You beast!" Adam teased.

"Oh, yes." Jack dropped all his body weight on top of Adam as he recuperated.

"Christ, you're crushing me." Adam tried to inhale deeply. "Jack, you're a sex fiend."

"Ahhh, that felt good."

"A testosterone filled macho man. That's what you are."

"You love it." Jack squirmed on Adam, squashing him even more.

"Ah! You're killing me!"

"You fucker, tell me how much you love it."

Adam lay still, then clutched Jack's rough jaw and brought him to his lips. Kissing him, wanting to show all his love for this man in that kiss, Adam sucked at Jack's tongue and felt it swirling around his mouth in dizzying patterns. Jack reached his hand down Adam's shorts. In the heat of their sweat, Jack exposed Adam and began jerking him off. Hearing their breaths echo in the metal and glass room, Adam rose up to the clouds, feeling his body levitate as it reached its climax. Clenching his jaw at the intensity of the orgasm, Adam grunted, hearing it ricochet off the walls. Gasping for breath, when Adam opened his eyes, Jack was rubbing his handful of come all over Adam's tight muscular belly.

"What are you doing?" Adam asked, panting.

"Smearing your come all over you."

"Kinky boy."

"Oh, that's nothing. You have any idea the fantasies I have about you?"

"Fantasies?" Adam perked up.

Jack stood, dragging Adam with him. Adam peered back at the mat and noticed it had Jack's sticky come on it.

Tripping up the stairs, Adam followed Jack, curious about what he wanted to do. Jack stripped off his shorts, hard as a rock again, and dug through the nightstand for a rubber. Finding one, then the tube of lubrication, Adam was gripped and yanked back to the gym once more.

"What the hell are you up to?" Adam stumbled behind Jack, trying to keep up.

"Get up on that bench. No. Take off your shorts first."

Adam slipped them off, trying not to be distracted by the wall of mirrors. "You're ready to fuck again? You just came? Just how much male testosterone do you have in you, Jack?"

"Too much. Especially after I work out. I always used to ejaculate after weightlifting. And you make me feel like I'm twenty again, Mr. Lewis." The rubber on, the lube dripping, Jack said, "Right. Get over here."

Adam stood still on the bench, waiting. Jack picked him up. "Wrap your legs around me."

"Standing? You're doing it standing?" Feeling Jack's cock inside him, Adam blinked in surprise when he found his way up and in. The minute Jack had penetrated, he face them to the mirror.

Adam began laughing, but he couldn't help looking at the sight of them, naked from the waist down, screwing.

Jack arched his back for balance and bounced Adam up and down on him gently. Trying not to be distracted by the sight of Jack's massive thigh muscles twitching from the power, Adam waited to see if Jack could climax a second time. Seeing Jack's eyes glued to the reflection of them in the mirror, Adam felt Jack's body tense up. "Go for it, babe!" Adam coached. "Come on, come. Fuck me. Come!"

Feeling Jack's hands grip his ass cheeks tight, Adam quickly brought his gaze back to Jack's. His eyes had closed and his cock throbbed.

"You amazing, man!" Adam gasped. "Sure, you're

thirty-eight, Jack, sure."

"I'll be thirty-fucking-nine in two days."

"No kidding? Well. We need to do something special for you."

Jack walked them over to the bench and allowed Adam to climb on it so they could disconnect. Pulling off the rubber, Jack moaned, "Christ, now I'm completely spent."

"No shit! Well, if you set out to impress me, you have!"

"I need a shower and to lie down."

Laughing the whole way behind him, Adam reprimanded him, "That's what you get for showing off."

Chapter Thirteen

Two weeks later, Adam and Jack were waiting for Mark and Steve to show up for dinner.

"You sure he's coming?" Jack asked.

"No, I'm not sure. Steve said he worked in a bookstore in Redondo. He's actually the owner of—"

"Shh, I hear them at the door." Jack rushed to open it.

Mark and Steve entered the room, waving and smiling at them. Steve handed Jack a six-pack of beer. "Got the brewskies."

"Thanks, Steve."

"So, what's going on?" Steve asked. "Mark said it's a birthday celebration for you, Jack."

Jack caught Mark's wink. "Uh, sort of. My actual birthday was a week ago."

"Oh." Steve appeared disappointed. "Why didn't you say something, Mark?"

"We sent him a card." Mark sat down on the couch.

"Did we?" Steve asked. "Oh. Happy Birthday, Jack."

Adam left the room. When he returned, he was carrying a box. Jack watched Steve's face as Adam set it in front of him.

"What are you doing, Adam?" Steve asked. "Isn't that for Jack? For his birthday?"

"No. It's for you. I know it took a while for us to do this, but all three of us wanted to thank you."

"For what?" Steve looked around the room.

"For what?" Mark shook his head. "Are you thick or what?"

"No, guys, really. What did I do?"

"You saved my life, Steve." Adam reminded him.

"That was weeks ago."

"Well," Jack explained, "it took us some time to get your gift together."

Sitting up, Steve looked at the box, "What is it?"

"Open it." Mark sat on the floor next to him.

Steve tore open the brown paper. Pulling open the flaps he reached in and took an item out. "Holy shit! Are these for me?"

"Yup." Adam winked at Jack. "I think we did good."

"Just wait," Jack reminded. "I'll get us some beer."

"Is this the whole collection?" Steve shouted.

Jack returned with four beer bottles. "As far as we could tell. We looked everywhere for them."

Mark added, "EBay, used bookstores, old websites."

Steve began piling the VHS tapes next to the box. "Oh, boy, oh, boy!"

"You still think he's better looking than me?" Mark kidded, smiling.

"Er, yeah. Sorry, Mark." Steve gave Mark one of Mark's classic pouts. "You mad?"

"No. But I will be jealous."

"Don't be. We'll watch them together and screw like bunnies after."

Jack whispered to Adam out of the corner of his mouth, "When's he coming?"

"I hope any minute."

"Did he promise?"

"Yes."

"What are you guys whispering about?" Steve asked. "You want to watch one? I haven't seen this one." He held up a movie with the word *Shame* written on it in balloon letters.

"Sure, Steve." Mark nodded.

When the doorbell rang Mark, Steve, and Adam exchanged knowing grins.

Steve sat up, "Pizza? Could I be that lucky?"

Jack went to answer the door. "You may be very lucky."

"Beer, pizza, and Loveday movies. It don't get any better than this!" Steve sucked on his bottle of beer.

Jack turned back to watch Steve's face as their guest came in.

"Steve Miller?"

Steve's eyes widened and he went completely mute.

"So, we meet again. I hear you're a hero and saved this man's life." The long-haired man gestured to Adam.

"Oh, my god. Angel! Angel Loveday!" Steve jumped to his feet and reached out his hand. "I'm so glad to see you again."

"Congratulations, Steve. Your friends know what a big fan you are and contacted me at the bookstore."

"It was the least we could do." Adam smiled.

Angel added, "I want you to know, Steve, there's no better man than one who sacrifices himself for others. You should be very proud of yourself."

"Mark," Steve shouted, "that is Angel Loveday."

"Yes, Steve, it is." Mark smiled sweetly.

"Can you stay? Have a beer?" Steve asked.

"I can't. I'm meeting my partner for dinner. I just wanted to stop by and congratulate you. I see you have worked out the other problem we discussed a few months back."

Glancing at Mark wryly, Steve replied, "Yes. He's mine. All mine." Steve winked at Mark. "Oh, can you autograph one before you go?" Steve held up a video.

"Sure."

Adam found him a pen. Jack loved the look on Steve's face while Angel signed the copy of one of his videos.

"Here you go. Good luck to you guys. Nice seeing you again, Steve."

"Thanks for making the effort," Adam replied. "It really means a lot."

"I'm just shocked anyone still watches those old movies. Anyway, see ya!"

They shouted goodbye. Jack closed the door and looked back at Steve's expression.

"Mark?"

Mark giggled. "Yes, Steven?"

"Was Angel Loveday just here?"

"Yes." Mark covered his mouth to stop his laughter.

"Fuck, he looks good." Steve dropped back down to the chair. Then meeting one set of eyes at a time, Steve said, "Thank you. It was amazing to see him again."

"No. You are amazing," Adam replied.

Mark snuggled on Steve's lap. "You need to fill me in on that little drink you two shared that you conveniently neglected to mention."

"It was nothing. I purchased a book from the store he worked at. We struck up a conversation and I invited him out for a drink. We talked about you and your relationship with Sharon. That was it. I suppose he was just allowing me to vent."

Mark's pout appeared, "Oh, then perhaps I don't want to hear about it." Mark nuzzled into Steve's cheek. "Do you still think I'm pretty, even compared to beautiful Mr. Loveday?"

"Oh, yes. Don't worry about that."

"Movie time!" Jack bellowed, taking a tape from Steve and putting it into the player.

Adam dimmed the lights. As Jack and he nestled on the couch, they could hear Steve whisper, "Mark?"

"Yes?"

"Thank you for getting Angel Loveday to come by."

A round of laughter circled the room.

"Thank Adam."

"Wow. Thanks, Adam. The guy gives me goose bumps whenever we meet."

"Well done," Jack whispered into Adam's ear.

"Christ, I'd have gotten a night with him if I could have. I owe Steve so much."

"No. It was perfect. Thanks, Adam." Jack kissed him.

"Shh!" Steve hissed. "Movie's on!"

Exchanging smiles, Adam and Jack snuggled up on the sofa watching Angel Loveday on the screen.

As the night wore on and everyone's conversation was mixed with yawns, Mark and Steve headed home while Jack and Adam cleaned up the beer bottles and Chinese food containers. Once the living room was in an acceptable state, Jack gestured for Adam to come upstairs for bed.

Adam followed him, his body feeling fatigued from all the exercise, sex, and long hours of work. Shutting off the lights behind him, and turning them on as he went, Jack began stripping for bed.

After Adam washed up and was under the sheets, he snuggled next to his lover and smiled. "You know, it was destiny we met."

"You think?"

"Yes. Look how much we accomplished together. You're back on good terms with Mark, I'm no longer in any type of danger, the fact that you and Mark have reconciled has led us to Steve, who in the end saved my life. Fate."

"Wow. That's some storyline."

"Yeah? You want me to find a producer to make a movie of it?"

"Nah. Who would you get to play me?" Jack stopped him. "If you say Dolf Lungren…"

"I wasn't!" Adam chuckled. "But I do love you, He-man."

"I love you too, Adam."

"Goodnight."

"Goodnight, lover."

The End

Coming Soon...
Book One of G.A. Hauser's
MEN IN MOTION SERIES:

MILE HIGH

Divorced accountant Owen Braydon spends his weeks working in Los Angeles and his weekends in Denver with his daughter. Straight-laced and mild mannered, he normally looks at the weekly flight to and from Denver as an opportunity to get some extra work done. But then he found himself on the same plane as the luscious Taylor Madison.

Texas-born Taylor is from Denver, but for several months he's been flying back and forth to Los Angeles where he works as a project manager on a major construction job. Charismatic and confident, Taylor is a man who knows what he wants and isn't afraid to go after it. The second he lays eyes on bi-curious Owen, he knows he wants him.

What starts out as a smoldering no-strings-attached initiation into the Mile High Club quickly turns into a weekly ritual that both men look forward to over all else. Soon their desire for one another deepens and both men find themselves wanting and needing more.

When a possible change in work assignments threatens to end what they have, both men are faced with a decision. Can the heights they soared together in the air be maintained on the ground? Only if Owen and Taylor are willing to cast aside their doubts, open up their hearts, set aside all inhibitions, and go the extra mile.

About the Author:

Award-winning author G. A. Hauser was born in Fair Lawn, New Jersey, USA, and attended university in New York City. She moved to Seattle, Washington where she worked as a patrol officer with the Seattle Police Department. In early 2000 G.A. moved to Hertfordshire, England where she began her writing in earnest and published her first book, *In the Shadow of Alexander*. Now a full-time writer in Ohio, G.A. has written dozens of novels, including several best-sellers of gay fiction. For more information on other books by G.A., visit the author at her official website at: www.authorga.com.

Also by G.A. Hauser:

Love you, Loveday

Angel Loveday thought he had put his life as a gay soft-porn star of the 1980's behind him. For seventeen years he's hidden his sexuality and sordid past from his teenage son. But when someone threatens Angel's secret and Detective Billy Sharpe is assigned to his case, he finds himself having to once again face them both.

Since his youth Billy Sharpe has had erotic on-screen images of Angel Loveday emblazoned in his mind. Now Angel is there in the flesh, needing his protection and stirring up the passionate fantasies that Billy thought he'd long ago abandoned.

As the harassment continues and the danger grows, Billy and Angel become closer. What began as an instant attraction turns into an undeniable hunger that unlocks Angel's heart. It's a race against time as Billy tries to save the man of his dreams from a life without love and the maniacal stalker hell-bent on destroying him.

To Have and to Hostage

When he was taken hostage by a strange man Michael never expected he'd lose his heart…

Michael Vernon is a rich, spoiled brat with a string of meaningless lovers and an entourage of superficial friends. With no direction in life, he wastes his days spending his father's money and drowning himself in liquor…until he crashes into a man even more desperate than himself, Jarrod Hunter.

Jarrod Hunter grew up on the wrong side of the tracks. Out of work, about to be evicted, and unable to afford his next meal, Jarrod thought he'd reached the end of his rope and was determined to take his life. Then fate intervened delivering him Michael Vernon. Why not take him home, tie him up, and hold him hostage to get the money he needs?

Two men from two different worlds…one dangerous game. Trapped together in close quarters, Jarrod and Michael find themselves sharing their deepest thoughts and fighting an undeniable attraction for each other. As the hours tick by, the captor becomes captivated by his victim and the victim begins to bond with his abductor. This wake up call might prove to be just what Michael needs to set himself free. To Have and to Hostage…sometimes you have to hit bottom before realizing that what you need is standing right in front of you.

Giving Up The Ghost

The visit from beyond the grave that changed their lives forever…

Artist Ryan Monroe had everything he wanted and then in a blink of an eye, he lost what mattered most of all, his soul-mate, Victor. Tortured by an overwhelming sense of grief and unable to move on, his pain spills out, reflected in the blood red hues of his paintings.

Paul Goldman thought he'd found the love of his life in Evan, his beloved pianist. Their mutual passion for music was outweighed only by their passion for one another. They were planning a life-time together, but then one fateful night Evan's was taken. Drowning in sorrow, unable to find solice, the heart-broken violinist has resigned himself to a life alone.

Now it's two years later and something, someone, is bringing them together. Two men, two loves, two great losses…and one hot ghost. Giving up the Ghost by G.A. Hauser, you won't be able to put down!

Capital Games

Let the games begin…

Former Los Angeles Police officer Steve Miller has gone from walking a beat in the City of Angels to joining the rat race as an advertising executive. He knows how cut-throat the industry can be, so when his boss tells him that he's in direct competition with a newcomer from across the pond for a coveted account he's not surprised…then he meets Mark Richfield.

Born with a silver spoon in his mouth and fashion-model good looks, Mark is used to getting what he wants. About to be married, Mark has just nailed the job of his dreams. If the determined Brit could just steal the firm's biggest account right out from under Steve Miller, his life would be perfect.

When their boss sends them together to the Arizona desert for a team-building retreat the tension between the two dynamic men escalates until in the heat of the moment their uncontrollable passion leads them to a sexual experience that neither can forget.

Will Mark deny his feelings and follow through with marriage to a women he no longer wants, or will he realize in time that in the game of love, sometimes you have to let go and lose yourself in order to *really* win.

Secrets and Misdemeanors

When having to hide your love is a crime…

After losing his wife to his best friend and former law partner, David Thornton couldn't imagine finding love again. With his divorce behind him, he wanted only to focus on his job and two children. But then something happened, making David realize that despite believing he had everything he needed, there was someone he desperately wanted—Lyle Wilson.

Young and determined, Lyle arrived in Los Angeles without a penny in his pocket. Before long, however, the sexy construction worker nailed a job remodeling the old office building that held the prestigious Thornton Law Firm. Little did Lyle realize when he gazed upon the handsome and successful David Thornton for the first time that a door would be opened that neither man could close.

Will the two men succumb to the tangled web of societal pressures placed before them, hiding who they are and whom they love? Or will they reveal the truth and set themselves free?

Naked Dragon

Police Officer Dave Harris has just been assigned to one of the worst serial murder cases in Seattle history: The Dragon is hunting young Asian men. In order to solve the crime it's going to take a bit more than good old-fashioned police work. It's going to take handsome FBI Agent Robbie Taylor.

Robbie is an experienced Federal Agent with psychic abilities that allow him to enter the minds of others. You can't hide your secrets and desires from someone that knows your every thought. Some think what Robbie has is a gift, others a skill, but when the mind you have to enter is that of a madman it can also be a curse.

As the corpses pile up and the tension mounts, so does the sexual attraction between the two men. Then a moment of passion leads to a secret affair. Will their love be the distraction that costs them the case and possibly even their lives? Or will the bond forged between them be the key to their survival?

The Kiss

Twenty-five year old actor Scott Epstein is no stranger to the modeling industry. He's done it himself between acting jobs. So when his sister, Claire, casts him in a chewing-gum commercial with the famous British model, Ian Sullivan, he doesn't ask any questions. He's a professional. He'll show up, hit his mark, say his lines, and collect his paycheck. Right?

Ian Sullivan is used to making heads turn. Stunningly handsome, he's accustomed to provocative photo shoots where sex sells everything from perfume to laundry soap. Ian was thrilled when Claire Epstein cast him in the new Minty gum commercial. He has to kiss his co-star on screen? No problem. Until he finds out Scott is the one he has to kiss!

Never before has a commercial featured two men, kissing on screen. Claire knows that the advertisement will be ground-breaking, and Scott knows that his sister needs his performance to be perfect. As the filming progresses and the media circus begins around the controversial advertisement, the chemistry between Ian and Scott heats up and the two men quite simply burn up the screen. Is it all an act? Or, have Ian and Scott entered into a clandestine affair that will lead them to love?

For Love and Money

Handsome Dr. Jason Philips, the heir to a vast fortune, had followed his heart and pursued his dream of becoming a physician. Ewan P. Gallagher had a different dream. Acting in local theater, the talented twenty-year-old was determined to be a famous success.

As fate would have it, Jason happened to be working in casualty one night when Ewan was admitted as a patient. Jason was more than flattered and surprisingly aroused by the younger man's obvious attraction to him. The two men entered into a steamy affair finding love, until their ambitions pulled them apart.

Now, one year later and stuck in a sham of a marriage that he entered into only to preserve his inheritance, Jason is filled with regret. Caught between obligation and freedom, duty and desire, Jason finds that he can no longer deny his passion. He plans to win Ewan, Hollywood's newest rising star, back!

A Question of Sex

Sharon Tice seems to have it all. She's beautiful, confident, sexy, and holds an executive position in her father's prestigious firm. But when her father puts her in charge of his latest building project, Sharon soon discovers that her life is missing something…Mark Antonious Richfield.

Mark is one of Los Angeles' most eligible bachelors, charming, charismatic and successful. His first encounter with Sharon takes him by complete surprise. The attraction between the two is undeniable and when they give in to the impulse to satisfy it, and one another, it's positively explosive.

After his first taste of Sharon, Mark is left wanting more, and the sultry blonde is more than willing until she's introduced to Jack, Mark's roommate, and begins to suspect that they are lovers. Somewhere between rumor and innuendo lies the truth. Will Sharon put aside her fears and jealousy long enough to discover the possibility of love? Or, will it simply remain *A Question of Sex*?

This is a publication of
Linden Bay Romance
WWW.LINDENBAYROMANCE.COM

Recommended Read:

Captain's Surrender by Alex Beecroft

Ambitious and handsome, Joshua Andrews had always valued his life too much to take unnecessary risks. Then he laid eyes on the elegant picture of perfection that is Peter Kenyon.

Soon to be promoted to captain, Peter Kenyon is the darling of the Bermuda garrison. With a string of successes behind him and a suitable bride lined up to share his future, Peter seems completely out of reach to Joshua.

But when the two men are thrown together to serve during a long voyage under a sadistic commander with a mutinous crew, they discover unexpected friendship. As the tension on board their vessel heats up, the closeness they feel for one another intensifies and both officers find themselves unable to rein in their passion.

Let yourself be transported back to a time when love between two men in the British Navy was punishable by death, and to a story about love, about honor, but most of all, about a Captain's Surrender.